UNLEASHED

Bone Frog Bachelor Series

Book One

SHARON HAMILTON

SHARON HAMILTON'S BOOK LIST

SEAL BROTHERHOOD BOOKS

SEAL BROTHERHOOD SERIES

Accidental SEAL Book 1

Fallen SEAL Legacy Book 2

SEAL Under Covers Book 3

SEAL The Deal Book 4

Cruisin' For A SEAL Book 5

SEAL My Destiny Book 6

SEAL of My Heart Book 7

Fredo's Dream Book 8

SEAL My Love Book 9

SEAL Encounter Prequel to Book 1

SEAL Endeavor Prequel to Book 2

Ultimate SEAL Collection Vol. 1 Books 1-4 /2 Prequels

Ultimate SEAL Collection Vol. 2 Books 5-7

SEAL BROTHERHOOD LEGACY SERIES

Watery Grave Book 1

Honor The Fallen Book 2

Grave Injustice Book 3

BAD BOYS OF SEAL TEAM 3 SERIES

SEAL's Promise Book 1

SEAL My Home Book 2

SEAL's Code Book 3

Big Bad Boys Bundle Books 1-3

BAND OF BACHELORS SERIES

Lucas Book 1

Alex Book 2

Jake Book 3

Jake 2 Book 4

Big Band of Bachelors Bundle

BONE FROG BROTHERHOOD SERIES

New Year's SEAL Dream Book 1

SEALed At The Altar Book 2

SEALed Forever Book 3

SEAL's Rescue Book 4

SEALed Protection Book 5

Bone Frog Brotherhood Superbundle

BONE FROG BACHELOR SERIES

Bone Frog Bachelor Book 0.5

Unleashed Book 1

Restored Book 2

SUNSET SEALS SERIES

SEALed at Sunset Book 1

Second Chance SEAL Book 2

Treasure Island SEAL Book 3

Escape to Sunset Book 4

The House at Sunset Beach Book 5

Second Chance Reunion Book 6

Love's Treasure Book 7

Finding Home Book 8 (releasing summer 2022)

Sunset SEALs Duet #1

Sunset SEALs Duet #2

LOVE VIXEN

Bone Frog Love

SHADOW SEALS

Shadow of the Heart

SILVER SEALS SERIES

SEAL Love's Legacy

SLEEPER SEALS SERIES

Bachelor SEAL

STAND ALONE BOOKS & SERIES

SEAL's Goal: The Beautiful Game

Nashville SEAL: Jameson

True Blue SEALS Zak

Paradise: In Search of Love

Love Me Tender, Love You Hard

NOVELLAS

SEAL You In My Dreams Magnolias and Moonshine

PARANORMALS

GOLDEN VAMPIRES OF TUSCANY SERIES

Honeymoon Bite Book 1

Mortal Bite Book 2

Christmas Bite Book 3

Midnight Bite Book 4

THE GUARDIANS

Heavenly Lover Book 1

Underworld Lover Book 2

Underworld Queen Book 3

Redemption Book 4

FALL FROM GRACE SERIES

Gideon: Heavenly Fall

NOVELLAS

SEAL Of Time Trident Legacy

All of Sharon's books are available on Audible, narrated by the talented J.D. Hart.

ABOUT THE BOOK

Armed with new focus and passion for restoring his rightful place atop his shipping, consulting and private security empire, former Navy SEAL Marco Gambini takes his new love on a dangerous and romantic pre-honeymoon to the Pink Pasha on a private island owned by the Sultan of Bonin.

Shannon Marr is up to more than just being Marco's sexual distraction and future bride. She inserts herself into the mission being planned to protect two of the Sultan's sons as they endeavor to grow their development business in West Africa.

The stakes are high but the rewards, both physically as well as emotionally, are worth it. Shannon is determined to earn her keep by helping Marco claw his way back up on top by exposing the strengths of her soft and warrior-strong womanhood. Together, if they can survive and overcome their new enemies, their partnership could be unstoppable.

Or they could go down in flames together.

Best read in the following order: Bone Frog Bachelor, Unleashed.

This series involves the same couple: former billionaire and Navy SEAL Marco Gambini and his new love, Shannon Marr, as they traverse oceans and play in the dangerous world of assasins and mercenaries while clawing their way back from the brink of destruction, restoring Marco's powerful fortune earned through his successful shipping, real estate and protection businesses. With each book in this series, Shannon grows into the partner he's always wanted: someone worthy of his trust as his right-hand woman, as well as the woman who can match him in every way in the bedroom.

AUTHOR'S NOTE

I always dedicate my SEAL Brotherhood books to the brave men and women who defend our shores and keep us safe. Without their sacrifice, and that of their families—because a warrior's fight always includes his or her family—I wouldn't have the freedom and opportunity to make a living writing these stories. They sometimes pay the ultimate price so we can debate, argue, go have coffee with friends, raise our children and see them have children of their own.

One of my favorite tributes to warriors resides on many memorials, including one I saw honoring the fallen of WWII on an island in the Pacific:

> "When you go home
> Tell them of us, and say
> For your tomorrow,
> We gave our today."

These are my stories created out of my own imagination. Anything that is inaccurately portrayed is either my mistake, or done intentionally to disguise something I might have overheard over a beer or in the corner of one of the hangouts along the Coronado Strand.

I support two main charities. Navy SEAL/UDT Museum operates in Ft. Pierce, Florida. Please learn about this wonderful museum, all run by active and former SEALs and their friends and families, and who rely on public support, not that of the U.S. Government. www.navysealmuseum.org

I also support Wounded Warriors, who tirelessly bring together the warrior as well as the family members who are just learning to deal with their soldier's condition and have nowhere to turn. It is a long path to becoming well, but I've seen first-hand what this organization does for its warriors and the families who love them. Please give what your heart tells you is right. If you cannot give, volunteer at one of the many service centers all over the United States. Get involved. Do something meaningful for someone who gave so much of themselves, to families who have paid the price for your freedom. You'll find a family there unlike any other on the planet. www.woundedwarriorproject.org

CHAPTER 1

MY DRIVER DROPPED me off at her Tampa television station, TMBC, so we could head to the airport after Shannon's last airing. I was a few minutes early. The original plan, which had been changed so many times I was having a hard time keeping track, had been to have a quick meet and greet with her parents before the two of us flew off to the Maldives. From there, we'd take a helicopter flight to the Sultan of Bonin's posh little island. Legendary for its pink sand beaches and pink exterior architecture, it was rare anyone from the West or even Europe would stay there. But my contract with the sultan to provide a security team for his sons during their African housing development project opened doors everywhere, including Washington.

At the last minute, I'd had to rush off to New York to settle affairs and to begin the shutdown of my Manhattan offices. I had initiated staff changes after the resignation of half my financial team and hired a new CFO. I planned a relocation to the Tampa area to be closer to Shannon's job at the television station, the Trident Towers project, and the construction of our new home on the Gulf Coast. Manhattan didn't suit me any longer. I was ready to make new memories, with Shannon.

My advanced security team were already on their way to meet us in the Maldives, which would be our base of operation. But Shannon and I would be the guests of the sultan, not far away.

I'd missed the lunch reservations with her parents due to the last-minute shuffle. Today, I considered it to be the most important meeting of my life. Better late than never.

Mr. and Mrs. Mabry sat in the Green Room. The large, noisy concrete-floored warehouse-type space resembled a cafeteria led to the main sound stage. Several make-up rooms adjoined, a few in use. I knew a more intimate studio existed for special interviews.

The two of them looked smaller now, grey-haired and seated side by side. They had not aged well and, seeing their profile from the rear, appeared frailer than I remembered them years ago when I'd been engaged to their oldest daughter, Emily. While I had been off being a Boy Scout on my first of many SEAL Team missions fifteen years ago, she'd tragically died in a car accident. Shannon had been a teen. This was going to be a difficult meeting for them.

Several large screens played live feeds from Tampa, as well as a couple of their affiliate stations in other locations in Florida. One wall was covered in vending machines—the only source of food or drink at the station. The chairs were old, and the couches were lumpy. Rolling set backgrounds had been stored there as well, which could be used to change the stage quickly for TMBC's various programs.

I approached the old leather couch from behind as they studied the screen with Shannon's beautiful face plastered five feet wide above them.

I placed my hands on their shoulders softly, careful not to scare them, and then slipped around and sat down next to them.

"I am the one to blame for not being here when you arrived. But we're delighted you could come. It's been a long time. And now you live in Florida. How wonderful." I spoke carefully, examining the lines on their faces and watching for reaction.

I held my hand out to Mrs. Mabry first, who was closest to me. Then to Shannon's father. Shannon was the spitting image of her dad, and I'd forgotten that. His piercing blue eyes evaluated me quickly, and I wasn't sure I'd passed the test. But her mother gushed, even blushing and touching my leg with affection, completely nervous, like her daughter would have been in this situation. Way back then, I never felt they blamed me for Em's death, but there was no doubt that my presence reminded them of those horrible years right after they'd lost her.

Shannon's mother spoke first.

"Delighted to see you again. Oh, Marco, it was such a long time ago. Even back then, we heard so many wonderful things about you. We've followed your career, all the amazing things you've done. What a busy man you are! Last we saw you was when you went off to become a decorated Navy SEAL. Em was so proud of you. We were too. *Are* proud of you." Her smile was genuine, although awkward, but I still didn't want to take advantage of it. I wasn't going to slick over or whitewash their feelings. Loss hurt, and pain wasn't going to disappear just because we re-connected or even because I was going to marry their other daughter. It would take time, perhaps lots of time.

"Truly, I am sorry." I nodded to both of them, individually. "All this was very last minute, as I'm sure Shannon's told you, and we couldn't put off the trip any longer."

"Is it safe where you're going?"

Her father asked the question I would have asked. He'd already lost one daughter, and I'm sure it was top on his list of things to worry about.

I nodded, not breaking eye contact. "Well, sir, there

really isn't any place on this planet that's safe any longer." I shrugged. "Probably never was. But people hire me to protect them, so I think she's in good hands—as long as she follows the rules. But you know Shannon."

I gave them a half smile. Mrs. Mabry reacted immediately. "Oh, indeed! Headstrong—"

"Bull-headed," her father added.

"Definitely has a mind of her own," her mother continued. "She loves adventure, though. I'll give her that. You'll have your hands full, I'm sure."

"I love her independent streak, rather like me. I love everything, even the stubborn parts. It will be pure pleasure to show her some of my world. I promise it will be an adventure, but we'll make it as safe as we can."

"So this is India?" her father asked.

"Not quite. Bonin is an independent island nation. Many of the other older kingdoms have been brought into the Maldives proper or rejoined with India over the centuries. Other countries, as well. But there are only six independent kingdoms left. Used to be hundreds dotting islands all over the Indian Ocean. Most of them eventually went bankrupt and sold to huge hotel chains or wealthy corporations. The sultan is a good manager of his assets and has taken care of his little kingdom well." I added, "And he knows how to keep good friends."

Mr. Mabry scowled and shook his head. "And now he seeks to expand to Africa? Nigeria, is it? That's sure not a place I'd go to set up business."

"Not exactly. He's doing a housing development, sort of a joint project with the U.N. and with a little underwriting from Uncle Sam. But it's a legitimate development investment for profit. I'm private security."

"Because it's so dangerous." He nailed me with the truth. I wasn't going to lie to him.

"North Africa is one of the most dangerous places on the planet. And there's much work to be done to help its people progress into the twenty-first century. But not to worry, sir, Shannon won't be going with me there."

He shot back a blank stare which gave me a chill, some kind of premonition, but I shook it off. Mrs. Mabry laughed, wringing her hands and straightening her skirt.

"Would you like anything?" I stood and motioned to the machines.

"We already ate. If I drink anything now, I'll be up all night long," her father said, rather glumly.

I was concerned he didn't approve of me. I knew I'd have to be patient and hope that he'd eventually come around. But that obviously wasn't going to be this evening.

"How was the Oceanis?"

"Big," he answered. "It must have cost a fortune."

"Well, as you've seen, you'd have been sleeping on an air mattress and sleeping bags at Shannon's."

He shrugged his shoulders. "We didn't mean to put you out. It was just for an overnight."

"And you deserved to be comfortable."

I was trying. Shannon had warned me about being on my best behavior, to get rid of the fangs and claws I sometimes showed when being challenged. But this was different. Everyone grieves in their own way, and I had mine.

Standing in front of them, I felt like I was giving a lecture, but the words had to be said. I pressed my palms together. "I just want you both to know how happy Shannon has made me. I had hoped that we could spend a lot more time together. And I should have asked your permission before I proposed, but I guess I was a little stubborn too. I didn't want her to get away."

Mrs. Mabry abruptly looked down at her lap. I'd made her cry, and it pained me. I knelt in front of her on one knee, placing my hand gently on her shoulder.

"I'm so sorry. Truly, I am."

When she looked up at me, her tears spilled over her cheeks. "Just take care of our little girl. She's all we have left, Marco. Life is fragile. Sometimes too short."

I carefully leaned forward, asking permission, and hugged the frail woman tightly. She resisted at first, and then I felt her muscles soften, and she allowed me to support her as I tried to show her how much love I had for her daughter. It was one of the most uncomfortable things I'd ever done.

Mr. Mabry stood with his back to me. I knew he'd been affected too.

As I drew away and rose, I wondered if this was just one thing too many we had tried to jam into our lives before leaving. I scored it as a mistake or wishful thinking on Shannon's part, and I wished I hadn't let her talk me into it.

Shannon entered the room, abruptly stopping when she saw the three of us standing like tongue-tied cows watching a train go by.

"Oh my gosh. What's happened?" she asked.

I let her see my worry over the conversation I'd just had with her parents.

"Did we have an argument?" she asked.

"Shannon, you were wonderful!" her mother said, completely ignoring the comment. Her father stoically hugged his daughter a second.

Shannon put her hands on her mother's shoulders and stared. "Mom. What's the matter?" Then she scowled at me.

Well, I guess I deserved it.

"It was rather more emotional for your mother than she expected," said Mr. Mabry, but his voice broke in the process.

"I see. Well, all that's over now." She tipped her mother's chin in the air as if Mrs. Mabry was the five-year-old and Shannon was the mother. She spoke directly to her face. "Mom, this is supposed to be a happy time. We don't have to live in the shadows of the past. We've done that. This is a new chapter in this family's life. Like I said, a happy time. I don't much care for the other one. I think we've done that enough."

"Well said." Her dad put his arm around his wife's shoulder. "Marina, you're raining on the happy couple's news. We should celebrate that."

Mrs. Mabry shot him a coarse look.

"I've got just the thing," I said, remembering he'd battled with alcohol all his adult life. There were several mineral waters in an undercounter refrigerator. I brought out four frosty bottles and opened them one by one, handing them to everyone. "To the love I share with Shannon and the many years of marriage we'll have together."

I held mine up, and we all toasted. Mrs. Mabry gave me a grateful smile. Shannon was at my side and whispered so softly only I could hear, "Thank you."

CHAPTER 2

WE FLEW FIRST class to JFK and then boarded a non-stop charter to the airport at Male in the Maldives. It was going to be a twenty-one-hour flight. By the time I got there, I would be so confused about the time of day it would take me several days to catch up.

We'd been escorted by a handsome uniformed attendant, who carried our on-board luggage, while a cargo crew brought several containers and stowed them in the baggage compartment. We mounted the stairs, and Marco introduced me to the cockpit crew, readying to take off. They were cheerful and appeared to be friends.

"Nice to meet you, Shannon. Glad to see someone finally grabbed hold of this guy before he gets too old to move. He's been rather elusive," the older of the two said.

"He surely is," I agreed. "But I think I got him just in time. I like silver foxes."

They both laughed. The younger pilot saluted Marco and put on his headgear.

"How does it look?" Marco asked the other pilot.

"I think we should have a fairly smooth flight. No big storms in the Atlantic, a little turbulence of the East coast of Africa, but nothing we can't avoid," came the answer.

The attendant asked us to do a quick tour to make sure everything was as Marco had ordered. "As soon as you're ready, we'll take off," he said.

I'd never been on a private jet before, and I never expected to be on such a big one, either.

The plane was leased by one of Marco's companies, a converted and upgraded Airbus for private commercial use. No expense was spared, with all-leather massage recliners and marble topped tables clustered here and there between them. A large table sat just in front of the galley, which was well stocked with enough meals and snacks to support a team of ten. A small bathroom was located there as well.

"We share this with the crew, but we also have our own. You'll see," he said as he wiggled his eyebrows.

Behind the kitchen was a large entertainment suite where we could watch or listen to anything we wanted on several big screens at once.

"We've got movies, internet—anything you want," he said.

In the rear, he showed me a private bedroom suite with a bathroom completed by a shower and a soaking tub decorated in white marble. The large king-sized bed was covered in brightly colored silk pillows.

He shrugged. "I had them add some, like you have at home. Just thought you'd like it."

Draped over an easy chair in the corner were two matching terrycloth robes and slippers.

"It's beautiful, Marco. You've thought of everything." I was truly stunned.

"I told you private jet travel wasn't like anything else in the world. You'll be so spoiled; you'll never take a commercial flight again."

"Are we ready?" the attendant asked from the doorway.

We took our seats, side by side, strapped in and held hands.

"A little champagne perhaps?" the attendant asked, handing us two flutes.

"Why not?" I said as I grabbed mine and passed one to Marco.

I leaned back and put my feet up on the leather ottoman while the attendant strapped in. As we sipped our champagne, we heard the engines roar to life, and soon we were taxying down the runway and then up into the night's sky.

After we leveled off, our attendant brought the bottle of champagne over in an iced stand. "What else can I get you?" he asked.

Marco waited for me to answer.

"I'm not very hungry. Maybe some fruit, some cheese, and crackers? Nothing heavy," I answered.

"Did you bring that seafood chowder I like?" Marco asked.

"Of course we did, Marco. You want me to heat some up? Shannon?"

"That would be great."

As he exited to the kitchen, I turned to Marco. "Never in my whole life did I expect to be doing this."

He finished his champagne and poured us both another one.

"You haven't seen anything yet, Shannon. Wait until you see the sultan's palace. It will blow your mind."

The attendant placed two steaming bowls of chowder on the table he moved to our chairs, along with a platter of fresh fruit, crackers, and cheese.

"Thank you." I hardly knew where to begin. "Everything is so lovely. Do you travel like this all the time?"

Marco shook his head. "Absolutely not. Sometimes it's a real bare bones deal, a red eye out of some place in a hurry. I occasionally have to stay twenty-four hours in the same set of clothes, even soaking wet. Depends on what I've been doing and how fast I have to get out of Dodge. But I thought tonight would be special. It was important to me."

How could I have ever doubted him? The more time I spent around him, the more I became convinced that his ex, Rebecca, was a complete whacko. How in the world would anyone discard him, even for millions? She'd had it all, I thought. And she blew it.

"You're awfully serious," he said, feeding me a strawberry.

"I know. It's just that I know you've had some setbacks recently, and you are juggling a lot. Are you sure you can afford all this?"

"I got a sizeable retainer. I'm good for a while. I have new projects in the pipeline. We're simplifying the office, so I'll save money there being in Tampa instead of Manhattan. The belt tightening is all good, Shannon. I'm not taking risks I don't think I can overcome."

"But with all the things Rebecca is pulling…"

"I think she's still shopping for another attorney after the last one quit. I just have to work a little harder, Shannon. In a way, it's a good thing. I've had to pay attention to more things now, because I can't afford to make mistakes. But I don't mind. I'm used to the pressure. It was a mistake to be so angry all the time. It dulled my sword for a bit. No more."

"But she really screwed you."

"She hasn't won yet. Sure, she got some things, but I think I might get them back and then some. That's the plan anyway. And, if not, it's not going to stop my forward momentum. That has nothing to do with her. It has everything to do with us. All she got was money. Stuff I can earn back. I got you. That's what I really wanted."

We kissed, and boy, did he light the flame! Maybe it was the champagne, but I wanted him so badly I was about to climb onto his lap in front of our attendant.

He leaned back and eyed me suspiciously, forming that little smile that drove me wild.

"Whatever are you thinking, Shannon?"

"Guess," I whispered.

"You didn't finish your chowder and only nibbled a bit on your fruit." His eyes were dark, serious. His aftershave clung to me. My chest was heaving. I was unabashedly totally turned on by him and wasn't in the least bit afraid to show him.

"Say something, Shannon," he said as his lips brushed against mine.

"Guess. And it has nothing to do with food."

He drove his eyebrows up into his forehead. "Ah, I see. I was going to pretend I am being slow to catch on, but I don't think I could hold myself back either."

"I'd see right through it, Marco." My forefinger caught on the top button of his crisp white shirt. I flipped it open.

At the second button, he sighed, giving our attendant a sheepish smile. "I think we'll go in the back and watch TV for a bit," he said.

"Of course. I'll clean up. Just buzz if you need anything."

I was working on the fourth button and hadn't looked at anything else but his tanned, muscular chest and the silver chain with the old Spanish coin attached to it.

He picked me up, and I waved good-bye to our attendant as he carried me to the bedroom, closing the door behind him.

I was tossed on the bed. While he undressed, I removed my dress and everything else except the very expensive lace panties and enhancing bra I'd purchased for the trip. He noticed. They were specially designed to make my chest look double, almost obscenely larger my normal size, which wasn't small. I loved his reaction.

He slipped a finger under my panties at my hip and pulled them to my ankles, but he left the bra in place. His thumbs smoothed over the white lace material as he bent down and kissed me. Moving a pillow under my hips, he took my hand and pressed it against his erection while he carefully teased the moist petals of my sex until I was wild with need. I tried to push down onto his fingers. He kept moving away, teasing me.

I squeezed his package, stroking him, begging him to enter me, but he continued to wait, watching my eyes, drinking in the lust rippling through my body. My libido spiked when I saw him dip his head, looking at me one last time before he dove into me, filling me with his tongue and fingers. His thumb found my nub. He brought his head up to watch as he pressed it, and I began to shatter beneath him.

I was already on the verge of an orgasm, but when he lifted my knee over his shoulder, angled his hips, and plunged inside, I was completely undone. I gasped for air as he nibbled my neck, kissed my ear, and bit my earlobe. He whispered my name as his fingers laced through my hair, pulling me up to his mouth. He kissed me then let me down gently and rode me harder. He was so deep. He grabbed my buttocks, forcing himself deeper still, rocking his hips as I pushed back, embracing his charge and giving him resistance. My internal muscles gripped him and would not let go as he moved back and forth, picking up speed.

I could no longer control the movements of my own body. My brain exploded into a thousand points of light as he held me tight against him, lifting me up by slipping a knee beneath my rear as we peaked together.

I stared into his eyes, unashamed that I needed him so much. We held this embrace until our breathing returned to normal.

He pushed the pillows off the bed, pulled back the silk coverlet, and wrapped us both in it. With my head buried in his chest in the warm cocoon we'd made, at over thirty-five thousand feet in the air, I was completely spent.

And I was completely his.

CHAPTER 3

I AWOKE AS rays of sunshine poured in one of the bedroom windows I'd forgotten to shutter last night. I slipped on some pajama bottoms, wrapped myself in the robe, and slid into the slippers provided. Leaning across the bed, I pulled down the shade so Shannon could continue to rest.

We'd nuzzled around off and on during the night but finally turned in under the covers to go to bed proper. I knew she was tired, and I wanted to make sure she kept her strength since we'd be in a much warmer climate than Florida's. Along with the foods and dust from the land, she'd get exposed to lots of new things. I exited the bedroom, leaving the door closed behind me, bringing my laptop. I wanted to work on some reports I was expecting from my new CFO.

I set everything up at the conference table, connecting a dedicated printer/scanner/fax I had stored in the upper compartment just in case I needed to send, receive, or obtain a paper copy.

Our attendant slept soundly, but he awoke when the pilot, Ron Hansen, entered the cabin from the cockpit. I'd previously worked with Ron when we both were in the Navy. He was part of a crack SEAL delivery team. He and his men had gotten us out of a lot of close calls back in the day, and I always relaxed when I was able to book him for these trips.

"Marco, everything to your liking?"

"I can't complain, Ron."

We shook hands. He used the head, and I went back to examining my reports.

When he returned, he asked, "You want some juice or a coffee?"

"I'll take an espresso. You making one for yourself?"

"Yup. I need a little caffeine right now. I can't nap for another four hours."

The espresso machine was loud, and I was concerned the high-pitched squeal might wake up Shannon. I watched the bedroom door for signs, but it remained closed.

Ron brought me the dark, frothy goodness in a little ceramic cup. Even on the plane, I insisted on using the Murder and Hate Espresso blend from my favorite veteran-owned coffee company.

He smacked his lips. "Wow, that's good. I gotta hand it to you. You don't scrimp on the details," he said as he toasted me and sipped his coffee again.

"Details, details. Very important, as you know."

"Roger that."

"She's in good shape?" I asked him, referring to the plane.

"You've got an engine running borderline hot. I'm watching it. I've got your crew meeting us when we land to check it out. Hope that was okay."

"Safety first. No problem here. I trust my guys."

"That said, I don't think it's anything to worry about. She's an older gal, but she purrs real good."

I smiled. "You let me know."

"Will do." He returned to the galley. "Another?"

"I'm good. I want to get back to bed if I can. Unless something snags me here," I said, pointing to my computer screen.

"You don't take these trips very often anymore. Been what, three years since we've been in the Maldives together?" he asked me.

"I've been doing mostly domestic things or government contracts, and hey, they pay for the plane, so yeah, it's been a while."

"What brings you back here? Understand you're doing work for the sultan?"

"He's an old friend, and I'm helping his boys out.

Never say never. You know how it is."

"I truly do. What's he up to?"

"This is preplanning. The boys are off to Africa for a housing development project. I guess that makes me bait."

Ron chuckled.

"How are the wife and kids?" I asked. He'd met his wife while in the Navy, and I recalled they had a whole handful of kids.

"Had a bit of bad luck there. She's out finding herself, but unfortunately, she took the kids with her. I'm working as much as I can. I'm going to be paying for braces, college, and then weddings all within the next five years. So I'm saving up."

"I'm sorry to hear that. But you didn't get divorced?"

"We wrapped it up. It's final, but it was clean. You know how it is when you were on the Teams. They want someone at home more. Kids don't grow up by themselves."

"I hear you."

"How about you?"

"You didn't hear about Rebecca?"

"I was being polite, Marco, letting you tell me what you wanted to and no more."

I chuckled. Score one for Ron. "I'm glad you don't read the papers."

"Your Shannon's nice. A future Mrs. Gambini?"

"She has a ring to prove it. Did you ever meet Em back in Coronado?"

"Don't think so."

"I dated Shannon's older sister. When I went off on my first mission, Em was killed in an auto accident. A drunk driver hit the girls. It was pure luck we ran into each other," I lied. "I met Shannon again after fifteen years."

"What are the odds of that? Did you know when you met her?"

"Didn't have a clue. I'm kinda glad it worked out that way too. I don't think I could have touched her if I'd known. Back then, she was all braces and huge glasses, a skinny little thing but very sweet. She grew up well."

"I'd say. When's the date?"

"Just happened, so we're working all that through. Just got re-acquainted with the parents again before we took off. I'm locked and loaded, Ron. Hopelessly snagged. And you?"

"I think I'm going to just focus on being single, trying to get in my dad time, whatever I'm allowed. But I'm looking."

We smiled. I'd always found him to be very easy to be around. He had his world of expertise, and I had mine. He'd saved my life on more than one occasion, and I owed him my undying loyalty and friendship.

"If I find someone exceptional, I'll be sure to let you know, Ron."

"You're alright, Marco. I'm happy for you." He stood, setting his cup into the galley sink. "Well, I better get back." He held up a mineral water. "Pete's thirsty. Oh, and I wanted to verify, we got it scheduled for seven days downtime. Is that firm?"

"For now. Once I get to the palace and see what's involved, I'll know more. We'll make sure you get plenty of notice. Are you traveling off the island at all?"

"No, I don't usually do that. And with this engine thing, I'm going to hang around tight. Probably catch up on my reading and some rest. Might try the beaches. Been awhile on that score too."

"You never know. Shannon always says 'The Beach Heals Everything.' I believe her."

"I like that. See ya."

The tall, lanky former Navy man meandered back through the cockpit door, after greeting our cabin steward.

"You need anything, Marco?" he asked.

"I'm good. Just going to work here for a bit. Then I might turn back in."

"You let me know what time you want breakfast, okay?"

"Thanks. I appreciate that."

I dug into several emails my new CFO had sent last night. I was pleased that he was able to get me so many detailed reports. I'd asked him to do a forensic analysis of some of our cash flow leaks and large transactions in and out of the company. He'd identified several unusual line items and then given me more detail.

Someone had been undercutting my equipment pricing, selling my own goods to a third party and then keeping the profits. He identified a small team of salespeople who lived down in Virginia doing contract work. I wasn't sure which one of them was the leader, but I suspected all five of them were involved.

I wrote a memo freezing their purchasing ability, unless they got my permission first, and when I recognized who the customer was, I fired off an email asking them to call me. I suspected that the procurement officer for Homeland Security, who I knew quite well, didn't realize anything about this. It was an easy pickup for these guys. I'd allow the discounting to continue, but I wanted to keep the funds, not let it wash out. If the officer was not guilty, he'd call me. If he didn't, well, he just lost his good deal permanently and our friendship.

We'd had offers already on the office building in Manhattan, which relieved me greatly. My ex had way overspent when we did the building re-design. I'd had a hard time keeping architects and engineers on the project because she was so volatile. That was about the time I realized she had been slutting herself around, preparing for her cash infusion via the divorce. So good riddance to it and everything in it, including the huge interactive display of hot spots in the world, her pet project, in the lobby.

I had incurred a big loan on the building while buying her out, but the equity would be useful and, post-divorce, wasn't anything I had to share. I instructed my agent to accept the offer they thought was most promising, verify the qualifications of the corporation purchasing it, and then enter into an exchange escrow so I could start looking in Tampa. But I warned her, if anything looked out of the normal in any way, to get in contact with me. I didn't want to be tied up in a lengthy escrow with someone who couldn't perform.

My bottom line was improving but still not where it needed to be. When the job was finished with the sultan, which wouldn't be for another six months at least, I'd be in good shape and then some. But Rebecca had tied me up everywhere. I couldn't refinance anything.

I had to sell off two of my planes and enter into a partnership with another shipping company to take some of the heavy carry off my back. Maintaining the ships and crew was not something I had the time to monitor closely and required someone who could step in and do that job. My new partner had been in the merchant marine business for nearly thirty years, forced out with a nice cash buy-out of his contract when the owner he worked for retired and sold to a Chinese concern who brought in their own team. He drooled at the opportunity to work with me, especially since he didn't have to buy anything, just keep it working, floating, and manned.

Rebecca had managed to muck up the Trident Towers project to such a degree she was getting pushback from the neighborhood now with her re-design. Her approach was attractive but unnecessary, and I felt like she'd be looking to back out of it. She'd made herself a money pit, just trying to keep me from having something I believed in: housing for disabled Navy SEALs, right on the beach. Rhea, my manager at Bone Frog Development Group, gave me all the skinny, all the juicy gossip, including a very public firing of my former CFO who she'd stolen away from my company, Frank Goodman.

He'd lasted all of about three months. That wouldn't look good on his resume.

Frank's father had been one of my first early back-ers and was a smart man who taught me a lot about investing. His son had worked for the IRS for twenty years before I encouraged him to go private with me. Turned out, the old man was indeed the smarter of the two, and I was glad he hadn't lived to see what a mess his son had made of his career.

I scanned the other profit and loss statements and the indexes attached and was generally pleased with what I saw. He made some good suggestions on ways I could trim the fat but not have to endure a total haircut that would block my expansion. One of his first suggestions I even received as a bonus the day he interviewed with me. He advised me to sell the Manhattan building, and that was turning out to be the best thing I'd done all year so far.

Well, other than asking Shannon to marry me, of course.

I also sent an email to Harry, the sultan's social secretary and illegitimate son who had been raised in the U.S. with his mother, informing him when we expected to land and requesting several reports on the Africa project I hadn't received yet from the "boys," as I called them—the sultan's legitimate sons and his half-brothers.

I received a nice invitation to a grand opening of a new Eastern Bank & Trust building in Boston, with a personal note from my old nemesis, Mr. Rory Cullen himself. Something was clearly up there, but I'd let him stew and get back to him when I returned to the states.

Next, I reviewed three new proposals for security services in areas I had no interest in serving in the

Middle East. Although technically safer than Africa would be for the next twenty years, based on the number of U.S. deaths, I wasn't as familiar with the arena as I'd been when I was an active SEAL. The intel was so critical. Even when it was accurate, things could go all to hell. And it was difficult if you got into trouble, due to the language, and the fact that you were working for leaders the public hated, and arguably might even be criminals.

And with the age of electronic warfare and surveillance with drones, it was hard, unless you had a big backer, like Uncle Sam, to affect any safety measures. Missiles could go stealth and farther. Drones could pack lethal doses of firepower enough to blow up an apartment building or shoot an airplane out of the sky. Electronics were tricky when without a dedicated satellite net. It was an easy way for bad guys to come raid your bank account just by making a telephone call home. It was scary stuff, and not what I had been trained in.

Africa, as dangerous as it was, still required all the old school knowledge we used to use when we were first in the Middle East. It was all about luck, and nothing to do with sophistication. Whomever had the biggest surgical strike team and the best intel, with the possibility of escalating troop numbers for backup, won. I was going to try to do that without the huge backup numbers. And I relied on locals to give me the intel, which I'd learned how to read and who to trust.

I asked my assistant to send my standard rejection letter to each, and to indicate that I'd be able to entertain future work in the next eighteen to twenty-four months.

I also emailed Senator Campbell, letting him know when I'd be arriving, and reminding him of his generous offer for Naval support, should I need it, from Diego Garcia. I was traveling with a letter on his letterhead indicating I was a top-level friend of Uncle Sam, and that no reasonable ask for assistance should be refused. It wasn't on Naval letterhead, from the Commander at DG, which would have made it official, but as Chairman of the Senate Armed Services Committee, he had even more clout, in a strange twist of fate. Besides, his wife, Beth, was the First Lady's younger sister.

I closed my laptop and stared out at the clouds in the bright blue sky. We were flying above the dark green lands of the continent of Africa now, nearly halfway to the Indian Ocean. I felt pretty good about all the planning, albeit last-minute, for this trip.

But I knew, it never really worked out that way. Something always went wrong and went to hell.

And I was trained for the unexpected. That was how I survived.

CHAPTER 4

MARCO WOKE ME up, and if he hadn't, I probably would have slept all day. The drum of the engines seemed to lull me to sleep with their white noise.

I eyed the tub and frowned.

"Maybe on the way back," he said, prying me out of the bed. "The shower is nice. I'll even join you, if you want. But breakfast will be ready in a half hour. Brunch, really."

"First, you tease me with a little shower fun, and then you tell me we only have thirty minutes? That's so unfair, Marco."

"So sorry, sweetheart," he said, grinning. He lifted my nightie up over my head and spanked my bottom, so I'd head to the shower.

We made the most of our few minutes' escapade with the lemon shower gel. I loved letting him shampoo my hair. His hands were so strong, and transformed it into a great back and shoulder massage that turned my bones to rubber.

The bathroom even had an expensive hair dryer and a full complement of my cosmetics and creams. "You did this?" I asked as I showed him the contents of the vanity drawer.

"Guilty as charged. All I did was take a cell photo of it at your place and give it to my assistant. Check out the closet."

He'd stocked the tiny space with several beautiful dresses, hanging in padded bags so I could wear them without a wrinkle. I had slacks and tops and a ratty pair of jeans I knew I'd love.

"Even shoes?" I asked, looking down at my favorite brand of running shoes, walking shoes, and a pair of flats for evening wear. "You are incredible."

"I had a lot of help, Shannon. All I did was document it. I can't claim anything special here. Let's just say I hire and pay well."

"I can see that." But I silently worried if we could afford it.

I wore a casual pair of slacks and my pumps, along with one of my favorite embroidered tops from my suitcase. It was slightly wrinkled, but for breakfast and arriving for the first time in an island nation, I thought I was good to go.

Connor brought us a delicious crab and cheese omelet, coffee, and orange juice that looked fresh squeezed. Marco was examining my shirt.

"I'm going to have Connor iron that for you," he said.

"What's wrong with it? It's not too bad."

"You are expected to look and dress like the soon-to-be wife of a billionaire."

"But—"

"It's all impression. And nobody knows out here I don't have the billion any longer. We're working on it, right?"

I nodded.

"The point is, we never know who will meet us at the airport, sweetheart. They still have a royal family, although the country is run as a republic and the monarchy has no power, just tradition."

"They are independent, is that right?"

"Yes, a republic, but they did just re-join the British Commonwealth and have lots of ties to Great Britain. They have a duly-elected president. Since any of them or their representatives could meet us, we have to be prepared. It's a great honor to be greeted by any member of the royal family, who are also closely aligned with our employer, the Sultan of Bonin."

Our attendant brought me the robe to wear while he took my shirt to the bedroom and ironed it. Marco kissed the side of my cheek.

"Thank you. There's a lot to learn, but you're a fast

study."

"So where do I get to wear the shabby jeans? Those are actually my favorite of all the clothes you brought for me," I asked him.

"I'd say long walks on the beach at night." He winked at me. "I'm sure we'll manage to use them."

Several hours later, we landed in the middle of a turquoise paradise surrounded by the Indian Ocean. I could see the string of islands going both north and south. But surrounding every single one of them were concentric rings of turquoise waters bordered by white sandy beaches.

Connor helped me select some of the clothing I'd bring, including all the dresses in padded plastic carriers. I hefted my computer case over my shoulder and grabbed my carry-on items while he organized our heavier luggage.

A blast of warm wind hit me as soon as the cabin opened, and we descended the gangway. Marco thanked the pilots first and then followed behind. On the tarmac, a bevy of crew scurried around in orange jumpsuits, tending to the large bins in the storage hold, as well as securing the shutdown. I'd never heard their language, and even the lorries put-putted their tiny two-cycle motors, honking and hustling.

Marco grabbed hold of my arm and urged me toward a waiting black SUV with black tinted windows the crew was beginning to load up from the back. I checked behind me, and Connor was not more than three feet behind.

"No entourage?" I asked Marco.

"Apparently not. Boy, did they miss the boat. Now everyone here will be talking about that American movie star they missed."

"What gave me away?" I continued the ruse, raising my voice a bit to reach over the sound of the plane's engines.

"Why, your two handsome escorts and those big sunglasses, of course!"

Checking his physique from behind, he did kind of look like any woman's wet dream of a security detail with his huge shoulders, slim waist and hips, thick neck, and enormous corded forearms that held the bags as easily as carrying a piece of cardboard.

We bid farewell to Connor. I gave him a hug, not sure if that was appropriate, and he blushed. Marco handed him an envelope.

"Thanks, man. See you in seven days, or before. I'll stay in touch with Ron, and he'll let you know, okay?"

"You got it, Mr. G. Have fun you two." He gave me a wholesome wink and made my heart skip a beat.

Marco turned and headed for the vehicle in long strides, and I barely could keep up with him.

"Why don't you think they'd guess you as the VIP

guest?" I asked, after we jumped into the blissfully cool second row of the SUV. I noted that the doors were nearly six inches thick, even the windows.

"Because I'm the old guy. It's never the old guy, sweetheart." His eyes danced in the darkness of the car's interior, continuing the tease. He checked me out from my head to my shoes and winked again, adding an appreciative nod.

If his age and the gap between us bothered him at all, he didn't show it. He leaned forward and directed the driver in an Indian dialect. The driver nodded, pointing to a piece of paper he held in his right hand.

"You know Arabic?" I asked him.

"Some, but that was Maldivian."

All I could do is stare at him. He finally turned his head and feigned surprise. He was definitely messing with me, and I was falling for every single one of his little jokes.

"What?" he asked. "I know a little bit of a lot of languages. Helps to know if they're talking about you or they're impressed with something."

"How many do you know?"

He rolled his shoulder. "I think about a dozen, give or take. You lose it if you don't speak it every day. I'm rusty on a bunch of them."

"You're kidding!"

He leaned over, grabbed me by the waist, and

pulled me into him. "Oh, I'd kid about a lot of things but never about languages or sex, sweetheart." His raspy whisper made my toes curl. I was so ready for his kiss I was breathless.

"You okay?" he asked when we parted.

"It's the heat."

His eyes twinkled. "It is. It is that all right."

As we traveled, I watched the luxurious foliage with large hotels behind ornately carved gates as we passed down the gulf road to where we'd be staying tonight and meeting the rest of the team. Marco pointed out one enormous conch-colored Victorian hotel with a pair of guards in crisp white uniforms standing outside an enormous gate.

"The royal family stays there when they come. Several of the kids spent their honeymoons here."

"Really?"

"There's another one around the other side that is actually built on an island itself. Very private."

"These are all privately owned?"

"Oh, sure. The government is poor compared to its citizens. Some of the palaces and temples date all the way back to the 1100s. We'll try to tour a couple of them, where you can wear your shabby jeans, if you like."

"And if it's hot, can I go without a bra?"

He leaned over and whispered in my ear, "You better not. I'd be upset if you did."

Finally, we drove up a small hill, paved in exquisite inlay designs. A large gate automatically opened for us when we approached the outer grounds. Beyond the green foliage, I saw an enormous three-story building that was brand new, with balconies, verandas, and colorful canvas awnings everywhere. We drove through an avenue of flags from several dozen countries flying in the breeze. The driver pulled up to a spacious granite lobby area and opened the door for me first.

"Mum," he said in his Indian dialect.

Marco slid out next to me, slipped his arm around my waist, and tipped the driver, who bowed and said something back.

"Wait until you see this, Shannon," Marco said, pulling me up the rose-colored granite steps into a grand foyer lit by an enormous stained-glass ceiling depicting a jungle theme with flowers, birds, and turquoise water lapping on a white sand beach. It was the largest stained-glass window or ceiling detail I'd ever seen.

"We're staying here?"

"Not quite here. We have a cluster of bungalows built out into the bay on a jetty. Ours has its own swimming pool. But I have a special surprise for you.

I was actually somewhat exhausted from just hauling my computer and carry-on case. It was a relief when a young man in a red uniform took them from me and placed them on a cart. He offered to take

Marco's, but he declined.

He picked up two key cards and retrieved some messages while the rest of the luggage arrived. I didn't see the large trunks.

Taking my hand, we crossed the lobby area, lined with jewelry shops and very high-end clothiers. At last, we came to an outdoor covered walkway that appeared to stretch out into the calm Indian Ocean for a mile or more. Branching off in several places were clusters of mini houses, some with pools and some without. Marco unlocked the gate with his key card and then held it open for the baggage cart and the handler.

All five bungalows fed into a large pavilion in the middle. It wasn't yet dusk, but already a huge fire was burning in the firepit, encircled with silk pillows and ottomans. A gentle spicy mist infused the whole area with an Oriental-Arabic scent.

We had one last gate to pass through, and we were finally at our front door. He pushed it open and stepped aside so I could walk in first.

The view of the calm, light blue waters and white puffy clouds in the sky was stunning. Looking straight out, no land was visible. It was just ocean and sky. Our private swimming pool waited just outside a wide patio door to the left. Colorful futons and umbrellas were staged at angles all around the pool. The oversized living room also had a firepit in the center and an open kitchen, with a bedroom I mistook for the master.

"Come, I want to show you something," he said,

motioning for me to join him down a tile-lined curved staircase to the level below.

Which was *below* the level of the sea! Soon, I began to realize what he wanted to show me. The large king-sized bed of this master suite faced one glass wall, and on the other side of that wall was the private pool.

"Talk about a room with a view," I gasped.

"Maybe you could put on a show for me. I wouldn't mind."

I shook my head and laughed. "I wouldn't even attempt it. I'm not graceful in water."

"Baby steps, my love. We'll take it slow and do one wonderful thing at a time."

I was in his arms in a flash, grateful, happy, and so much in love.

"Thank you, Marco. I didn't even know any of this existed."

We kissed. "Truth is, Shannon, before you, it didn't really. Or if it did, I never saw it. It's fun because I love watching the expression on your face."

"Well, I'm just wondering how you could ever be happy lounging around my little house in Florida. After what you've seen and how you've lived? It's just incredible. That's all I can say."

He drew me to him again. "We're just getting started, Shannon."

CHAPTER 5

W E MET AT what I called the "common room," where a light dinner, consisting of local seafood delicacies and fruits, was set out for the team. We also had an open bar and refrigerated non-alcoholic fruit juices they used at the world-famous spa located on premises.

It was a job, but all three of the equipment trunks were brought in as well. We'd learned our lesson once, leaving those items on the plane on a past mission. We not only lost the equipment, but the hijackers took the plane as well.

One of the trunks had already been off-loaded and sent by ship to the sultan, chock full of his favorite wines from California, jeans and gifts for his wives and children, some electronic toys he didn't have access to for the grandchildren, two smoked turkeys, and half a dozen smoked hams. He wasn't allowed to have pork, but his obsession with the taste trumped his religious convictions. I was only too happy to feed his addiction.

The rest of the equipment I intended to have delivered to the boys once the paperwork was signed and the scope of the job was agreed to. But I had already been paid twenty-five percent of the overall fee, which I could keep if we didn't come to terms. I wasn't worried about that.

In the meantime, these trunks would stay with my team until we made arrangements for the sons to have them delivered. Since the importation of guns in regular luggage was forbidden, I had some weapons designated for my team in one trunk, signed off by Senator Campbell and agreed to by the sultan. I hadn't even carried my Sig, and I was feeling mighty naked without it. It was one of the first things I retrieved.

I introduced the three staff who I'd hand-picked for this preliminary mission.

"Shannon, this is Karin Atkin. She's got State Department experience but also is fluent in Arabic, several other African dialects, and a little Mandarin. Right, Karin?" I asked her.

She blushed and nodded her head. She had married an American, a Marine sniper, who was killed on a mission in Afghanistan several years ago, but she still kept her Canadian citizenship and passport. How she managed to get top security clearance without being a U.S. citizen was still legendary, and my attempts to find out were always rebuffed.

I noticed Shannon kept a close eye on her, since she was an extremely intelligent and beautiful blonde. They shook hands.

"Congratulations. I think you've got a wonderful guy here, if you can keep him out of harm's way."

Everyone but Shannon laughed.

I had gotten the hard one out of the way first so went on to introduce the other two. "My coms guy, Nigel Macron, builds drones in his spare time. I think he has an AI wife somewhere, but we don't know for sure."

Nigel shook her hand. "He lies through his teeth. Don't ever trust him," Nigel said as he gave her a wide smile.

"Nice to meet you, Nigel. You're from the U.K.?"

"Actually, the border country. Scots by birth. Most of my ancestors were inventing weaving machines when Marco's were herding cows."

"Watch it. You can't eat wool," I said. "What's the use of staying warm if you starve to death, Nigel?"

"You're terrible," Shannon scolded me.

"Smack talk. You start hanging around my people and you'll swear like a sailor in time. Doesn't take me long to get right back in the groove."

"And here you were talking about ironing my clothes. What a snob!" she reminded me.

All three of my guys howled at the gotcha. I knew I'd get even later on tonight.

"And finally, Forest Davis, who still holds the record at Florida State for the mile, or has that been shattered yet?"

"Almost. They're a couple of ticks behind but catching up." He stepped forward and shook Shannon's hand. "Very nice to meet you."

"Likewise."

During our meal, Shannon asked what other things the team was specialized in.

Karin began. "Asking permissions to go into foreign countries as an NGO takes a little skill at times, especially when governments are experiencing various degrees of instability. I try to stay in touch with the players. They know who I work for, and sometimes that's easier than if I was with Uncle Sam, looking to butt into some country's internal affairs."

"I can see that." Shannon asked another question. "Can you get denied in the middle of a mission?"

"Oh, we've been close but not yet. Most of these things, while sometimes surprises, can be worked out. And cash talks, too, when everything else fails."

"Karin is also an ultra-marathoner, and she's been on two Everest trips."

I'd embarrassed her, and she shrugged. "Sort of my life. No family, so I push myself," she said.

"Karin was one of my first hires."

I recognized great talent, and I had seen she was going to spin out of control after the death of her husband. Rebecca never liked her, but then Rebecca didn't ever like anyone who could potentially be held as a rival.

"I can see why. I'm very impressed. I can't do all of that, but I do like to jog a bit, and I'm good at floating on a blowup pink dragon on a pool somewhere warm, sipping on an umbrella drink."

"Now you're talking my style," said Forest.

"Shannon's the weather girl for TMBC television in Tampa. And I'm still trying to find those films she had parts in."

"Oh, don't!" said Shannon. To the group, she stopped suddenly. "It's not how he makes it sound. A couple of Indies, not porn films. Marco, where are your manners tonight?"

"I'd still like to see them. With or without your clothes on."

"It doesn't take much talent to get covered with blood and scream in a corn field. My part was not memorable, and the other one got cut out." She paused before looking at the next person. "And, Forest, what's your specialty?"

The handsome black former Marine Recon searched the ceiling before he answered in his most angelic tone. "Death."

Shannon did a double take.

"Explosives, firepower, poisons, knives—whatever I can use in the field to help break in or out of something quick. I help with the drones, too, and the communication equipment in general."

"He's also had a career in Mixed Martial Arts," I added.

Shannon commented, "I feel safer already."

We had a brief meeting, just like we used to do it on the Teams. I apologized for the lack of material coming from the brothers.

"Yeah, and that's not a very good sign. You have to make them understand, Marco. We can't protect them if they take a lazy attitude toward this," said Nigel.

Both Karin and Forest agreed.

"It's my biggest problem with this deal so far. And that's what I'll be evaluating when we meet."

"You going over tomorrow?" asked Karin.

"That's the plan. I've got Paul on standby to fire up Little Bird. He's been here for a month doing the safety checks, and he's told me we're good to go. Just waiting for the final okay, which I should get tonight. If not, we'll hang here a day with your guys."

"I researched the two towns in Nigeria and a bit of the region you said the project was going to be located. You're starting right at the beginning of rainy season.

Was that intentional?" Karin asked.

"Not my choice."

She nodded. "Well, we've got roaming bands of militia running from Chad and Benin, going back and forth across the border. It's a red zone, Marco. A U.N. certified red zone, the whole prefecture. You said they had permission from their regional minister?"

"That's what Harry told me."

"I'd sure like to see that chit, if you can get your hands on it."

"Got it," I said as I pulled out my little vest pocket notebook and wrote it down. "Any actions recently?"

"It's been pretty quiet the past six months," she said. "Sort of like an earthquake, though, the longer the time from the last one, the more likely the next one is right around the corner."

"Great. You're the queen of good news."

She smiled. "That's me. Keeping it real for all of us."

I appreciated that about her. The two men admired the comment as well.

"I got your sidearms and extra stuff in trunk number two, so help yourself," I said to the group in general. "What you ordered should be there. And, Nigel, I have your C4 and other shit in there too. In trunk number one, I've got Kevlar, Invisios, and the phone grabber. I brought the two drones you ordered, too, and a backup radio in case the SAT phone doesn't work."

"Santa has been good to me this year. Thanks, Marco. I know exactly what I'll be doing tomorrow."

"Watch out for that stuff, though. I don't want you bugging the tourists or interfering with air traffic with those things. Do it carefully."

"No worries." Nigel was rubbing his hands together eagerly.

"Karin, I'd like an assessment of how many men you think we'll need for the Africa trip, just preliminarily. I'll get more of the details to you after my first meeting on the island."

"I can get started, yup."

"Okay, gang. Rule here is they come in and leave your meals and supplies in the great room. So keep the trunks locked. Your rooms are all off-limits, but they'll leave your sheets and towels for you in here. If you need a cleanup, you have to request it. But no one is to bother you in the room. Oh, and breakfast is at eight-thirty. That was the best I could do."

I looked around at my little team, all different in builds and expertise, but all first class in their fields. We were to keep our room keys on us at all times, in the lanyard provided by the hotel. I knew by the time we were ready to leave, everyone would be good and fed up with having to swipe the gates so many times just to get access to their private spaces, but it was for their own safety. Unless there was a sea invasion, we'd be safe here, and the management was doing flip-flops to keep my business.

We said goodnight, and I took Shannon's hand, walking to our room. I needed a few minutes to check my emails for those things I'd demanded and not yet received. I halfway suggested she take a skinny dip in the pool while I was doing that. She wrinkled up her nose at the suggestion and retreated to the bathroom.

I opened my laptop and started reading over a report from Harry about the location of the project and the permits and approvals pending, which I forwarded to Karin's computer. He also confirmed the time we had permission to land, so I sent another email to Paul asking for him to deliver my Sikorsky and got quick confirmation he would.

I was studying a new report from my CFO when something caught my eye. When I looked up, Shannon was putting on a show for me in the pool.

I slammed shut my laptop and had my clothes off in about thirty seconds.

CHAPTER 6

THE BLACK SUBURBAN met us just outside the lobby of the hotel at ten o'clock, and three hotel staff assisted in loading up our suitcases and the long garment bag filled with my evening wear and a tux for Marco.

I was still glowing from the night we spent under the stars, both in and out of the pool. There had been jokes at our expense as the rest of the team chided us over breakfast, asking if we'd heard the pirates who had managed to break into our pool and patio area.

And here I thought we were being so quiet.

Marco had a perpetual smile on his face and didn't say a word, but he managed to slide against me, touching me in private ways several times during breakfast and afterward. I was finding him to be an even more affectionate man than I thought as I learned to read his little expressions and carefully crafted whispers and growls.

The tough, unflinching exterior worked well for him in his business dealings, but his intimate tenderness with me left my ears ringing, leaving me in a heightened state of sexual need for him constantly, day or night. The addiction I felt for his touch, his kisses, and mere presence of his powerful body had grown from the first time we were re-acquainted back in Boston only a few weeks ago. Our romance was stuck on one speed: fast and intense. My life before I met him faded into a pale background.

Vaguely aware that Marco's world completely overshadowed my own, I nonetheless welcomed all of it with reckless abandon. The more we were together, the more I wanted to be by his side. If there were any warning signs, they were completely shut down.

Karin slipped a printed report into his hands before we left, and he tucked it into his computer case as the Suburban took off down a crowded single lane freeway of sorts, toward the airport.

"Will all these bags fit?" I asked.

"Fit? You mean in my Little Bird?" His eyes nearly glowed every time he mentioned his special helicopter, a lighter version of the one the President of the United States had, he'd told me.

"Exactly."

"In a pinch, we can seat more than a dozen with gear. So no problem."

I couldn't imagine a machine so large, but as soon as we arrived, I saw the red and white two-toned bird with the BFI logo utilizing the frog skeleton discretely placed on the side. The pilot came out to greet us with a co-pilot left inside, which surprised me. Marco was right, the cab could easily hold a dozen or more passengers.

He held us back until the rotors began to turn, eyeing me carefully. He was of Indian descent, very handsome with dark skin and jet-black straight hair, making his white teeth look nearly fluorescent. In his jumpsuit and military-looking Aviators, he was the picture of a swashbuckling pirate most my friends would fall for, like one of the heroes from my romance novels.

He addressed Marco first. "Nice to see you again, Marco. Got all your messages," the pilot shouted over the sound of the twin engines.

"Good. Paul, I want to introduce you to my fiancée, Shannon Marr."

His eyes grew as the recognition of our engagement settled in.

"Shannon, this is Paul Vijay."

His handshake was warm, and firm. "Very, very nice to meet you, Miss Marr. Is this your first visit to the Indian Ocean?" he asked.

I could barely hear him, but I got enough of it to

answer one word. "Yes."

"Well, shall we get started then?" He motioned toward the helicopter.

"You had everything checked out?" Marco asked while we ducked under the rotors.

"Yes, yes. I have the report you can read inside. Very little trouble considering how long it's been since she's been used. It passed certification no problem."

"Excellent," Marco mumbled as he helped me up the step and pointed to a wide leather seat behind the pilot. The co-pilot gave me a brief nod and salute. Marco reached over his shoulder and shook his hand.

"Kenny. Thought they had you in the Caribbean this week."

"Someone else got it. That's okay. I wanted to spend some time in the Maldives with Paul, here. When I heard it was you, well, I had to come."

I was struck by the fact that, everywhere Marco went, his crew respected him and treated him warmly, whether they were his hire or contracted out by others. Everyone surrounding him were like brothers and sisters of the same family, and not a dysfunctional one.

I was probably being naive.

Marco placed a headset over my ears. An epic movie score type theme song was playing in the background, perfectly matched to my sense of adventure.

"Everybody ready?" Paul's voice asked over the com.

Marco gave a thumbs-up, and I nodded.

We rose straight up thirty feet, and then the front of the helicopter dipped as we accelerated and launched out over the ocean. The island's turquoise reef and white beaches were striking as we flew under a blue, cloudless sky.

"Music okay?" Paul asked.

I nodded.

"I'm going to turn on a little more air. Going to be hot today," he said.

Turning to Marco, I mouthed, "How long?"

He held up one hand with a four and the other with five fingers splayed. Forty-five minutes.

Slicing the deep blue of the ocean was a huge cruise ship headed for the Maldives. Other container ships and a large old-fashioned sailing vessel dotted the areas between a string of islands, all with the same turquoise rings, looking like a giant squash blossom necklace from the Navajo. As we traveled what I assumed was farther north, the shipping lanes disappeared and many of the islands we flew over appeared uninhabited.

He grabbed my hand in both of his, kissed my palm, and placed it on his thigh.

Paul turned slightly. "Did you see the Eagle?"

I wasn't sure what he meant.

"The three-masted cutter we passed earlier?"

I nodded.

"It belongs to the U.S. Coast Guard. They're doing trainings here, getting ready for a big international race next month. She's hoping to win this year, but there will be about fifty others—lots of competition. Beautiful craft."

I tried to talk, but it was useless.

About a half hour later, Paul pointed forward as an island with a wide bay and deep, pinkish-toned sand came into view. We must have been several miles still out to sea, but there was no mistaking the huge light bisque-colored palace with turrets and spires looming up from the lush jungle foliage in front of us. I felt like I was flying to Disneyland.

The pilots chattered to someone on the ground, who responded in heavily-accented English and signed off.

"Shall I do a three-sixty around, Marco?" Paul asked over the com.

He shook his head no.

An airstrip appeared suddenly as we descended between forests of palm trees just past the massive bay. The palace was completely obscured from view by the foliage. A pair of black SUVs waited next to the heliport hangar as Paul soft landed and shut the motors down.

Marco removed my headset and hung it on a hook at my side, securing it with a strap.

"Did you see the palace?" he asked me.

"How could I miss it?" I asked as the door opened and I was helped down to the concrete pad. "I looked it up, but the pictures I saw didn't look anything like that. The place is huge."

"I'm surprised you even saw a picture. You probably saw an old dummy photo of another palace. He's a very private man, for being so wealthy. I doubt he has more than a handful of real close friends."

I was counting my bags as Marco noticed something and straightened up tall.

"Here he is, Shannon."

I turned and watched a rather rotund older man appear through a line of uniformed and armed men, wearing golden robes that flowed in the breeze over white pajamas. His headdress material matched the robes and wound like a cloth crown about his enormous head. His wide, almost pure white handlebar moustache made him look like the perfect postcard picture of a sultan. With his arms outstretched, he greeted Marco warmly, kissing him on both cheeks.

His deep guttural voice cut right across the other noises of the airport.

"It's been too long, my friend. You traveled well?"

he asked Marco.

With his arm over my shoulder, Marco proceeded to introduce me. "Very well, thank you. We were in the Maldives last night, so we're rested and ready to get to work. Your Highness, may I present my fiancée, Miss Shannon Marr?"

The sultan fixed his gaze on me, his smile wide, enlarging the size of his moustache and revealing several missing teeth.

"Welcome to Bonin, my child." He opened his arms, and I was suddenly pulled towards him, smothered in a tight embrace. Knowing I wasn't used to the protocol, he turned my body by clutching my shoulders and kissing first one cheek and then the other. Just as fast as he grabbed me, he let go as I rocked back on my heels to keep from toppling.

"Oh, Marco," he said, winking to me with an obvious flirt. "You have such a pretty one. Beautiful."

"Thank you, Your Highness."

"My dear, you will make my wives jealous!" And then he gave a big belly laugh, turned, and gestured to the second SUV.

"Are your sons here?" Marco asked.

"Tomorrow. They went to Mumbai last week on business. But they return tomorrow morning. So we dine and celebrate until their return. It is good, *n'est pas*?"

His eyes twinkled as he twiddled his fingers in the air, showing off quite an assortment of jeweled fingers.

He didn't wait for Marco's response.

We sat in a seat facing the sultan, right behind the driver and another uniformed guard holding a small semi-automatic.

"Now, tell me all about your life since we last talked on the phone, Marco." Before Marco could begin talking, he interrupted. "You know, Miss—I'm sorry—"

"Marr. Shannon Marr. You may call me Shannon."

He cackled and cocked his head. "No, I will call you Miss Marr, or I will have trouble at the palace. Marco here is very, very smart and does not have fourteen wives. He marries for love and chooses with his heart. He is bitten by this snake, I think, yes?"

I hoped I'd not started an incident I'd be scolded for later.

"So you've told me," Marco softly responded, squeezing my hand.

"So what I was going to say is that this man is very special to me. He is like a son."

"Thank you, Your Highness."

"You are. And you are well trained and disciplined. The money part and all that stuff with Rebecca—I assume you know about Rebecca, yes?"

Before I could answer, he continued, "I remember you once told me this. That which doesn't kill you makes you stronger. Am I right?"

"You are correct, Your Highness."

"In a way, this little kerfuffle with her is a good thing. Otherwise, I have it on good authority you wouldn't have accepted my job offer. Am I correct?"

I could feel Marco's insides churning, even though he was doing a good job of masking it. I expected what he said next.

"For you, Your Highness, I would always clear the decks to work on a project. Sometimes, it's not possible. Depends on the contract I've signed, but yes, the timing was good and I'm available. That part was fortuitous."

"Fortuitous indeed, Marco. Good for both of us."

"Thank you. I agree," Marco said with a slight bow of his head.

"And good for you, my dear. What an adventure," he said with mirth, pressing his palms together.

I had wanted to watch the beautiful gardens and lush wild forests we drove through, but the sultan was an all-consuming figure who demanded our full attention. I picked up right away that he was used to getting his own way—not frequently but always.

"So come on, tell me," the sultan demanded.

"The most important part is that we are now officially engaged, and—"

The sultan held up his right hand, moving his fingers back and forth, demanding a look at my ring. I placed my hand there.

"Very nice," he said as he gently kissed my knuckles and released my hand.

I couldn't make out the look the two of them shared. In fact, I was sure I was missing half the nuances between the two men.

"And what else?"

"I have successfully sold the Manhattan building, or at least we're about to enter into escrow. Then I'm going to start looking in Tampa."

"You are moving from New York to Florida? Will you walk around in shorts and sandals now? Do you think this is wise?" At first, his stern look alarmed me. Then he burst out laughing. I presumed it was his way of telling us our lives were little and his was big.

He would be a dangerous enemy.

"I'd actually like that. Mostly, my business is done over the phone anyway, so what does it matter if I wore my red, white, and blue boxers?" Marco added with a smile, happy to play along.

"I don't blame you there. I used to spend long hours at the beach. Not so much now. I might get mistaken for a whale, and one of the fishermen would haul my carcass in with his net!"

I noted Marco lightly chuckled but was careful not to be anywhere close to the sultan's casual and overemphasized demeanor.

"Your office in Manhattan, I'm sorry to say, was a horrible fiasco. I never liked that place. Too cold and drafty. Sterile. Looked like it was designed by a German." His honest evaluation was duly noted. Marco agreed.

I would ask Marco later about the German comment but guessed it had to do with past history.

"So now you are about to start your new life. And babies. You'll want to have babies right away. We'll make sure while you're here that you drink our love potions that help a woman's belly to conceive."

I was shocked at the liberty he took with me, someone he didn't know, and my body. Marco squeezed my hand before I could blurt out something I would regret.

We arrived. Two guards on white horses and in red uniforms outlined in more gold braid than I'd seen anywhere stood on either side of the enormous palace's carved archway and doors. Above us, the many spires and towers of the palace looked down. I heard birds calling and smelled the delicate sandalwood scent of incense. Marco helped me out of the van as several aids scurried to take all our things inside. Marco kept his computer slung over his shoulder, but I gave them everything.

We stepped through the archway into a room that

was nearly three stories high, lined in blue and green tiles with colorful designs. There was a row of a dozen heavy columns several feet wide, all tiled, creating corkscrew patterns as they ascended up to the golden domed ceiling above. Tiny windows at the top allowed shards of light to pour over the inlaid marble floor. The colors, the detail, and the glistening gold of the great room were unlike anything I'd seen in any of the greatest cathedrals in Mexico or pictures of European churches.

"You like, my dear?" the sultan asked me.

"I'm speechless," I whispered back. It was the total truth.

The last couple of days had been more than I could have imagined. But this, this eclipsed even my wildest dreams and fantasies.

I felt like I'd stepped back in time by hundreds of years.

CHAPTER 7

THE SULTAN WAS a good study of human nature. He put Shannon and I up in the turquoise room, instead of the pink one he'd given Rebecca and I some years ago.

Attention to detail.

That's why I was hired, I reminded myself.

As Shannon stared aghast at the opulence of the wide stairways of marble and semi-precious stone, I had to grab her several times to avoid her knocking over a priceless urn or statue. The balcony-feel hallways leading to the guest rooms upstairs, overlooking the grand room entrance, were illuminated by the golden stained glass ceiling hovering above us all, as if Heaven itself was keeping a special, watchful eye on us mere mortals.

While she tried to take in everything, I watched her, enjoying the sense of wonder and awe I'd bet she had as a child. Nothing made me happier than seeing her in this state, far away from all the pressures of her life in Florida. At least, she thought she had pressures. In reality, she had no idea what the world was really like, and that this was all an illusion.

But I had too much love for her to take it away now, and so I observed how she absorbed the centuries of wealth and tradition, just like I had done some ten years ago when I first met the man who was more generous than any other I'd met and would treat me like a son, if I let him.

I actually thought of him more like an older brother—someone whose help he needed to keep his progeny alive as they put on their little water wings and tried to explore, to compete in the outside world. He and I both knew, as they approached their late twenties, they were both in danger of becoming hot house plants—raised in the stifling world of the sultan and his wealth and power, where work was not required. If they got in a jam with their studies in school, a first-class tutor could be flown over to bail them out. He wanted them to make their mark but not die trying. It wasn't important if they failed, as long as they came home alive.

My secret mission was not only to help them come home in one piece but have them come home in triumph. For that, prayers to the sultan's elephant god in my honor would be required every day by his entire kingdom.

He'd watched us climb the stairs, bidding us fare-well with a wave as I turned around and smiled. He'd asked permission for Shannon to attend a party put on by his wives and their attendants.

"I promise they will transform her, pamper her in luxury, and turn her into a harem princess fit for a king. You'll thank me, Marco," he'd said.

Shannon had frowned, not sure if she was going to accept, but I bowed and thanked him for his kindness. There wasn't a chance in the world I would let her pass up this opportunity, and it was as much for my benefit as hers.

Shannon's expression wasn't lost on the sultan as he gave a faint belly laugh and then motioned to the grand stairway, which was wider than Shannon's house, saying to our backs, "One hour then. They will collect her at your room in one hour."

I pulled Shannon behind me and gave her no room to turn around to give him the attitude I knew brewed inside her. One thing I had learned about Western women was that they were in such a hurry to achieve what their male colleagues had, even to surpass it, that they forgot sometimes the enormous power they had as a female. I'd told my men many times out in the field to watch out for the mothers and girlfriends, even the school-age girls, because they were the stronger ones in some of the cultures we fought in. They'd honed their strength by being oppressed for centuries. It wasn't fair, but it made them extraordinarily strong and difficult to challenge.

Shannon wasn't one who knew her strength yet. She was unblemished, relatively unscarred, except for the loss of Emily, which would forever be a basement emotionally for her. What I enjoyed was her light, her softness, and her ability to experience wonder and be happy. As she grew to learn the nature of her womanly power, I never wanted her to lose that quality. It would always be her secret weapon, bringing light to a dark world. Perhaps, she was my safety net, as well, if I ever got there.

She was the only woman I'd ever met that I would consider having a family with.

But all that would be hopefully coming at some future date. Right now, I had to explain the gift that was given her and convince her to embrace it, allow it to be something she enjoyed. Even if she was unsure or a tiny bit uncomfortable, she needed to keep her claws inside.

I closed the heavy door painted with scenes and designs from their culture. She marched up to the bed, because it was on a pedestal requiring three steps to reach the top, tossed her computer bag down on the satin tufted coverlet, and peered down at me.

With the backdrop of the carved four poster sandalwood frame wrapped in long, shimmering drapes, she was magnificent in her stubbornness and anger. I think the smile I couldn't help breaking out added to her emotional meltdown.

"Who does he think he is? Marco, there's nothing wrong with me. What is this, a Mary Kay meeting or something?"

I shrugged. "They just want to fix you up."

"Did I express to anyone that I needed fixing?"

"No, sweetheart, you did not."

"Then why didn't you let me refuse? I'm humiliated."

While she stood there with her hands on her hips, I made imaginary designs with my right foot, tracing the inlaid patterns of stone. "Because I think you'll enjoy it. It's a routine they do. They take great pleasure making each other look more beautiful."

"That's an awful custom. They're just objects of his desire. I want to be more than an object."

"Oh, they are far more than objects of his desire. They inspire him to be a great man, Shannon. He enjoys how they honor him by pleasuring him."

She abruptly looked away and sat on the bed, thinking. Perhaps I'd cracked a tiny part of her shell.

I added more, hoping she'd understand. "If you won't do it for fun—"

"Fun? That's not fun. It feels like a slumber party when I was a teen, where we'd talk about boys and—"

I knew what was going to come next. Em had told me. I wouldn't break the confidence, even though she was long gone. I remembered how she used to talk about dressing Shannon up, putting makeup on her, brushing her hair out, and making her look exotic at twelve, braces and all.

I mounted the steps slowly, watching her deal with thoughts I had no right to invade. But Em had told me so much about her, almost as if she had prepared me for the bride I would have, not the one I expected. My eyes filled with water as I watched hers overflow.

You are so like your sister, and yet you are so different.

Finally, she inhaled, wiping the tears off her cheeks with the back of her hand. "Go ahead," she said without looking at me. "You were going to say something about this being fun." Then she chanced a glance up at me. I sat next to her and took her hand.

Her hand gripped mine, knuckles white. I brushed the hair from her neck and whispered to her ear. "Shannon, become my harem girl, for just a night. Pretend what it would feel like to be a queen of an exotic and strange land where you are waiting for you prince to come claim you." I paused, feeling her tension disappear. "It's in your novels, Shannon. Go play a character in one of those stories. Pure fantasy, sweetheart. Let me be the hero to your heroine tonight." I kissed her as a follow-up and waited.

Her breathing was ragged as her emotions welled up.

"Say you'll do it for me, Shannon."

She nodded then returned my gaze. "Just when I think I know and understand everything about you, Marco, you come up with something like this that just blows me away."

"It's because I love you."

I lifted her chin, and we kissed. Her cheek pressed against mine, her hands around my neck, and the way she kissed had me in great anticipation of what was to follow. I knew the world for what it is, but for today, we'd make of it what we wanted.

Nobody in the universe would ever be able to take it away from us, either.

She leapt to action, escaping from my embrace, suddenly. She was at the bottom of the platform before I could stop her. "Marco, what do I wear? I should change my underwear."

I fell back on the bed, laughing.

"No, I mean it. Are they going to dress me in some saris and such? I should have my clean, newer things on. I just wanted to be comfortable today so wore my cotton—"

Tears streamed down the sides of my eyes, soaking into the satin coverlet. I could hear her unzipping her suitcase and ransacking her neatly folded things inside.

I came up on one elbow, watching the spectacle of her nervousness. "You are dressed fine, just the way you are, sweetheart. They'll do everything for you. I'm sure they'll dress you—everything. All you have to do is enjoy it."

"But you said I shouldn't be wrinkled, that I—"

I shook my head. She had misunderstood everything I'd told her. "That's different. That was on making a good impression to a head of state, someone who has a staff of more than two dozen to make sure he shows up impeccably dressed. It's a form of respect. This is different. The rules are different for the harem."

I got the look I deserved. With her hands back on her hips, she scowled. "And how do you know?"

I didn't want to tell her Rebecca hadn't enjoyed the encounter and had asked them to stop after the first few minutes. But she had good reason to not like stranger's hands on her body, with her past. That wasn't my secret to share with Shannon.

"Because I've had conversations with his sons, mostly Harry, his favorite, Shannon. But you—" I said, as I got up, descended the stairs and held her by the shoulders. "You'll have the first-hand experience, and you can tell me all about it. I want to learn about every detail."

She grabbed me and pressed her face into my chest. She mumbled into the fabric. "I'm such a klutz. You must think I'm the most clueless girl in the universe."

It made me sad to hear this. I gripped her tight, my fingers massaging her neck and shoulders and sorting through her long hair. I kissed the top of her head.

"Nothing could be further from the truth."

We heard a timid knock on the door, and I held her hand as I opened it to a bevy of lovelies, dressed in silks and jewels. The older woman in front bowed with her hands together. "If you would please do us the honor of lending us your wife, sir, we would be grateful."

"Of course."

Shannon's wide eyes studied the stunning ladies in front of her. I transferred Shannon's hand to the older woman and observed as they closed ranks around her, whisking her down the marble hallway with only the gentle swishing sounds of saris and tiny metal bells tinkling as they took her.

With another wife on her other side holding that hand, Shannon looked up at me from the top of the stairs, paused, and meekly smiled.

I blew her an air-kiss and watched them take her away from me.

CHAPTER 8

WHATEVER I WAS in for, I promised myself I'd try to enjoy the pampering. Searching from face to face, all I saw were beautiful women, from barely twenty up to Marco's age. They were stunning creatures, their shiny black hair worn in braids while jewelry dripped from their earlobes, wrapped around their necks, wove into their hair, and dangled down onto their foreheads. Their dark eyes were lined in heavy black charcoal.

Their saris sparkled in the light as we descended the grand stairway, walked down the marbled corridor decorated with granite, alabaster, and dark-veined marble statues of women in various states of undress. In between, every ten feet or so, another pair of carved columns supported a carved ornate Arabic arch decorated with paint and tile relief in varying designs. The ceiling above was blue, like a summer day in Florida, complete with clouds and occasionally a bird. Tiny windows let in beams of light through the hallway walls just above shoulder height, made with interconnecting filigree, ceramic tiled blocks.

My two monitors did not let go of my hands nor did they say anything to me. Others behind me whispered. I felt hands on my long hair, which I had secured with a clip. Someone made a remark, and another hand removed my clip. My hair fell to my shoulders.

Two young women opened a metal gate that had turned light green with a patina from centuries of use. I stood in the middle of a dome inlaid with tile, semi-precious stones, and gold. In the center, with three shallow steps down, was a turquoise pool covered by flower petals floating on top. Steam rose from the water, indicating it was warm.

All around the pool were settees and lounge chairs covered in long, brightly colored silk pillows. Several alcoves at the sides led to closed doors or revealed specialized workstations for massage. A tall, frosty refrigerator carried an assortment of fruit juices and a large bowl of fruit at the bottom.

Hands removed my shoes, storing them out of sight. Then my shirt came off. Someone else reached for the back of my bra to undo the fastener.

My spine stiffened as I scanned the circle of women that had formed around me.

"It's quite all right, mum," said one of the younger

wives, a pretty thing near to my own age. Her English was flawless. "You need to relax and just allow us to wait on you. We do everything for you."

My bra loosened, and my arms instinctively crossed over my breasts to hide them. Two women took hold of my palms, beginning a finger massage on them, applying oil and rubbing it into my skin as they lowered my hands to my sides while another woman unzipped my slacks and slipped them down over my hips.

Again, my reaction was to draw my arms back up to my chest, but my attendants continued my massage, holding my hands firmly in place at my sides.

Next, my panties fell to my ankles. The group moved away from me a step and called out things I couldn't understand, as they circled around me. I knew they were making plans, evaluating me, perhaps deciding what kind of treatment they would provide. They rubbed my elbows, felt the texture of my hair, examined my eyes, and no doubt found hairs on my upper lip I'd neglected to pluck recently. One woman held up my hand, studying my nails. Someone must have remarked that I had pierced ears because there was a light rumble of agreement to the discovery.

"You have a beautiful body, mum. We are going to make you look like a princess."

"Thank you." I didn't know of anything else to say.

"Your skin is dry, mum, so it needs a good exfoliation and then a yogurt masque. Your muscles are tight, especially around here…" She touched my lower neck and traveled along the top of my shoulder. "Your nails need painting. Your hair should be conditioned, and excess hair will be removed."

I was used to getting facials, so this didn't sound half bad. Nothing on that list bothered me.

"But first, you must relax and meditate. We must get your body ready to become the vessel it was created to be, so let us begin with a warm perfume flower bath while we prepare the other tables."

My clip miraculously appeared again, securing my hair up on the top of my head. Three of the wives dropped their clothes and led me naked down the steps into the pool and sat with me at the edges. A bucket was brought, filled with scented water. With large natural sponges, they sluiced the warm liquid over my shoulders, my neck, and both my front and back. Warm oil was poured over my skin as the sponges brushed and rinsed the oil evenly all over my body above my waist.

One of the three women was pregnant and just beginning to show. I pointed to her belly. The English-speaking woman answered my query.

"She is five months along. We will all celebrate the sultan's new child before the end of the year."

I smiled at her, but she turned her face away, covered her mouth with her hand, and giggled.

"You are outside the family. It isn't customary to speak of it if you are a stranger. But you come with Marco, who is like a son to our sultan. You do not know our customs, so all is forgiven."

I was directed to sit up at the lip of the tub as the oil and sponge routine was performed on my legs. One of them scrubbed the bottoms of my feet and between my toes, which tickled, and I jumped. She used a pumice stone on my heels, scrubbing with a coarse salt mixture made with yogurt and honey. The same treatment was given to my elbows, and then I jumped back in, and they sponged me off.

Next, I was directed to lie down on a cloth-covered massage table. A cool face mask was applied, allowed to soak for a bit, and then wiped off. Four hands carefully lathered and shaved my underarms and legs while a woman at my head waxed my upper lip and chin then wove tiny hairs into my brows.

At last, a warm face masque was applied, and my eyes were covered with a folded ice-cold washcloth. "You will try to sleep now, if you can. Just one little procedure first."

When I felt fingers down in my pubic area, I sat up, tossing the washcloth to the floor.

"Wait. What are you doing?"

"Have you not had this done?" she asked me, her large brown eyes showing concern.

"Once. I had it done once. But—"

"Mum," she started, laying a gentle palm on my shoulder, speaking in a soft lilting tone. "We endeavor to deliver you as hairless as possible. It will bring you both a great deal of pleasure. We have found that often it increases the man's ardor."

I wasn't worried about Marco's ardor at all. I was worried about the pain I knew was to come. I deemed it unnecessary, and I told her so.

"Mum, if you will just allow us to try. We have herbs that make the experience more pleasurable."

I doubted that. It was the reason I'd vowed to never do it again. It had been a dare in college.

"Just lay back and try to think about how smooth you will feel, like a baby's bottom, when we are finished."

The washcloth was replaced. More masque was applied as I lay back and felt a cold kind of gel being applied to the hair around my sex. Before too long, I realized it was a numbing cream. My knees were bent slightly and then spread wide as they applied the cooling gel up and down both sides of my labia. Within seconds, I felt like my female parts had been partially frozen, not to mention thoroughly examined. The gel was wiped away, and warm wax was drizzled over my skin as the layers of silk were pressed into place and then suddenly ripped loose. I was prepared for the worst.

I hardly felt a thing.

Greatly relieved, I could finally relax as they worked to make sure every hair was gone. They even held my knees to my shoulders and denuded my anal area.

The masque was peeled away, and a yogurt and honey mixture was painted all over my face and front, including my ankles and toes. Warm sandalwood oil was poured onto my scalp as strong fingers worked it into my hair and temples, giving me the best scalp and head massages I'd ever experienced. At the same time, my feet were drizzled in warm wax and placed into plastic baggies. They gently pushed them inside insulated cloth sacks smelling of lavender. They repeated the same thing with my hands.

"Time for a nap, mum."

"Okay," I mumbled, not daring to move.

I had no idea how long I slept, but when I started to feel the spray of warm water over my body, I remembered where I was.

Everything was repeated on my backside. The plastic bags were removed. Warm oil was poured over my back and legs and then a sheet applied to soak up the excess.

Someone's strong hands found every muscle pull, every place I held tension in my upper back, neck, and shoulder area and lovingly working it out of me while two or three others massaged the long muscles of my calves, thighs, lower back, and arms. The pressure was too firm for me to doze off, but when they were done, I could hardly sit up. I felt like a cloth doll.

My neck and shoulders were worked on from the front in the same process, pouring oil, soaking it up, and then working it into my skin. Even the soles of my feet were attended to.

I was moved to another station where I sat in a recliner, my feet propped up and given a thick juice drink, like a smoothie, with the most unusual color of rose red. It tasted delicious.

My English translator rubbed her belly and pointed to the pregnant woman. "Very good for welcoming a child."

The young wife nodded her head in respectful shyness.

"What is it?"

"Mother's milk from water buffalo, sweet beets, yogurt, and passionflower petals."

I sniffed the glass and could finally smell the gamey milk scent. Figuring it would be polite not to, I finished it off and asked for a glass of water to rinse my mouth with.

I was given a sparkling water with a lime in it, which tasted delicious.

She helped me lie back at the edge of the chair, lowering it over a deep sink and pouring more oil onto my scalp before wrapping my head in a hot towel. She placed sliced cucumbers over my eyes and waited several minutes before adding shampoo and carefully rubbing in circular motions until the mixture was lathered into a stiff peak.

I would never be able to tell him, but they gave me an even stronger, more thorough shampoo than Marco did. An herbal conditioner was applied, and again, a warm towel was wrapped around my head. I was moved to another station.

This time, I was directed to lie on my back on top of moist strips of silk. They had been soaked in chamomile, she told me. Gently, they wrapped me in these strips, my arms bent over my stomach, fully encased like a mummy. And then they wrapped me in a light-weight metallic blanket and strapped me to the table in four places.

"Time for another drink and another nap, mum," she whispered, holding up a glass with what smelled like apricot juice mixed with white tea and sprinkled with pomegranate seeds. I used a supersized fat straw and consumed every drop.

I fell asleep to the sounds of water splashing and

playful laughing.

Yup. I could get used to this all right. And just when I thought I'd floated off to Heaven, she placed a headset over my ears, and I listened to sounds of the waves at the ocean.

That's when I thought about Indian Rocks Beach and how the surf and the sounds of the sea birds had lulled me to sleep every night since I'd arrived and began to call it home. I couldn't help it, but I felt Marco's hand in mine as we walked the beach, watching the bright orange and yellow clouds turn purple and grey, as I allowed tears to drip down onto the table.

I missed my little place and the simple people there. I missed the decorated golf carts at Halloween and Christmas. I missed the firepits and the stolen kisses. I missed the way his body protected and warmed mine when we spent the night under the stars.

Did I have to come all the way over here just to find out I belonged somewhere else?

Maybe that was the point of it all—to experience something totally different and mind-numbingly beautiful only to find what I would come back to was even better.

CHAPTER 9

I REVIEWED SOME of the files Karin had printed out for me, studying maps from my SOF days back in Coronado. The Navy had never asked me if I'd turned off the software, so I continued to use it and figured I'd get the axe one of these days. Or maybe, someone purposely left it on for me.

But for now, it was a portal to some of the most accurate information I could get about our deployment schedules and, more importantly, why. It didn't tell me all the strategy or high-level decisions the senior chiefs would have with the president or his Washington team, but by watching what they were moving and when, I could put it together fairly accurately.

And there was a lot of concern about Nigeria, neighboring Chad, Mali, and others. While we focused on the Middle East, our friends in China had developed partnerships with many of the central African countries. And when I say partnerships, that meant an infusion of capital. We'd gotten stingy with our cash, demanding some of the leaders clean up their act, especially after Benghazi. Our public didn't have the stomach for things like killing ambassadors and troops who really couldn't do anything anyway but were getting murdered.

The bold strokes we made with our catch and grab routines in Afghanistan had worked for a time. What we'd lacked was the will to help those countries transition to a peaceful civilian-run government, based on good science, not voodoo economics. Wishful thinking got a lot of guys killed, and most of them were patriots like me. It was a sad story, Vietnam all over again. The only people who were saved were the ones who got airlifted out. The country was going to do what the country would do, and we could only destabilize it by inserting ourselves without concrete plans.

Oh, we did a good job, and we learned quick after Vietnam. A lot of our military leaders grew up cutting their teeth on these things and learned the hard way. Right after World War II and again twenty years after Vietnam, none of our Joint Chiefs had ever seen combat. There was a vacuum. They were learning in the war colleges from men who had never seen the hell of combat. Some of our boys paid the price until we got to take the training wheels off.

I didn't have the luxury of second-guessing all that,

and I didn't hold a grudge. I cared about it, and I cared about the guys we lost. But it wasn't my rodeo. I was punching tickets at the tollbooth, granting admission to the arena of war and training these boys so they could live to see another Christmas or get lucky in the back of their pickup truck when they got home.

But what made my project, the Trident Towers, so important wasn't that I was making these injured guys whole. I was giving them a chance at a somewhat normal life. I'd been damned lucky. I was paying it back for the ones who weren't.

It dovetailed nicely with what I did on the security front. Sure, I knew guys who liked to swagger around, telling everyone they were badass Navy SEALs so they could pick up chicks and be the kind of kid their parents would be proud of, especially after 9-11. They'd become personal trainers to the Hollywood crowd and fly on corporate jets with politicians and captains of industry. Every day before I got out, I heard those stories. And it made me sick. It was one of the reasons I couldn't do it any longer.

I wanted to be a captain of industry too. I'd earned my stripes and paid a heavy price for it, as well. I wasn't about to go take cushy jobs that looked more dangerous than they were. I wanted to do more than get those looks from boardrooms and Ted Talks. My ego didn't require that. I wanted to help the nonprofessionals cope with and see the real world for what it was: a dirty, evil place filled with people who would take away what wasn't defended, managed by desk jockeys and politicians who didn't have a clue. The empty shirts made good speeches and kissed babies. I wanted to teach *regular* citizens how to deal with these groups, how to help out the sorely needed populations of these war-torn countries.

Anybody could be a big guy when they're HALO jumping with thirty other lethal warriors at midnight who would die to keep you safe. I was dealing with the detritus, the part of the world who had to handle the aftermath when all the soldiers were gone, when they were fighting with rakes and shovels and slingshots. When their whole lives were consumed with protecting their kids as they went to school or their wives and daughters from traffickers when they tried to go to the store or hold a job. Dynasties like the sultan's could be overthrown in a heartbeat. He knew it, too. And when it came right down to it, for all his wealth, he was still a father and husband trying to protect his little brood.

No, I wasn't one of those who came crashing in with a new administration, cocky as hell, and not smelling my own shit. Because I knew the real truth of it.

Nobody *ever* got it right more than a small percentage of the time.

Nobody.

A gentle knock on my opened door caused me to look up.

"You are working? I thought you would come downstairs and we could wait together, have a little chat, Marco."

"I'm sorry. I was just taking advantage of a little quiet time. But you're right. I should have kept you company."

The sultan sat down in the overstuffed chair adjacent the table I was seated at. It was painful to watch him. Life was slipping away, right through his fingers. He wasn't able to buy himself another one.

"You work too hard, Marco," he said as he turned his bloodshot eyes on me. We studied each other silently before I answered him.

"Not sure I can do it any other way, Your Highness. I'm like you. I have a lot to do, a lot to live for."

He slowly nodded his agreement. I noticed his fingers were swollen, and there were purple patches around his ankles from lack of circulation. It wouldn't do any good to recommend he lose weight or start walking or riding a bike. Or avoid eating that magnificent honey-baked ham I brought him.

"I always thought it was Rebecca who drove you."

"Never. She was the sidecar, but in the end, she didn't inspire me. I don't think she ever did. She was a user." I pointed through the doorway. "Shannon inspires me."

"Ah, I do understand inspiration." He smiled. "Some people get it going to their Christian church, worshiping a virgin, unspoiled woman or a bloody corpse on a cross. My ancestors? They would have me worship an elephant with four arms, so fat, like me, he's pulled on a cart by his great friend, the rat. When I was a little boy and first began to read and watch television, I discovered the beautiful buildings in Rome and wondered why I had to worship an elephant and not some golden God in the sky above. That might have brought inspiration to me."

His story was funny, and I chuckled. I enjoyed seeing the world, or little glimpses of it, through his unique perspective. I would miss him when he left us. He would leave an irreparable vacuum behind. I appreciated the confidence he had in me to be able to show me his tender, mortal side.

"Highness?" a timid house attendant spoke from the doorway. "You wish anything to drink, perhaps?" I knew his English was for my benefit.

"You brought some of that California wine, didn't you?" the sultan asked me.

I got up and handed him the Cabernet he loved. It was from the winery founded by a famous director, and I'd described the tasting room that held so many famous movie props from the man's movie career to the sultan many times.

He held the bottle up, admiring it. "Someday, you will introduce me to this director, yes?"

"Definitely. You come to California, and I'll set it up. I think the two of you would get along. He runs a powerful kingdom too."

The sultan handed the bottle to the attendant, who quickly disappeared.

"Do you have any questions you wish to ask?"

"One thing I didn't see in the material they sent was copies of their permissions with the heads of state. I'm told there's a process and has to be sorted. I wanted to know how far they've gotten."

He wrinkled his brow. "We'll have to wait until tomorrow. I was told everything was in place. But they don't always tell me the truth. That's why I've hired you, to ask the right questions."

I suspected as much.

We were brought two wine glasses on a silver tray, along with the corked bottle. The attendant set it on the table. I moved my things out of the way, stowed my laptop, and tucked the confidential reports next to it.

He held his glass up when we were again alone. "To youth. Nubile, beautiful women and the inspiration they bring to our lives."

I could easily drink to that, and we clinked glasses.

"Hmm. That's so good. You know they tell me in Delhi they grow wine, but I don't believe it. Too rocky and dry."

"They made wine in Egypt, even found some in the great pyramids."

"Ah, those wizards of the heavens. They made wine out of anything. I mean *good* wine."

"Australia has a huge wine growing region. The Greeks did. And there are even wineries in Alaska."

"Not the same climate."

"True."

The looming thought between us was the women, who would be joining us in another hour or two. As if I'd pushed that into his head, he asked me about it. "You think she is enjoying this?" he said as he took another sip of wine.

"It's been over two hours, and she hasn't bail yet." I smiled. "Thank you for that, by the way."

"Oh, I am curious too. I haven't had so much fun anticipating this for a long time. I didn't want to tell you what they had planned until you got here so you couldn't back out."

"She's a pretty good sport. But I think she'll enjoy it, if she lets herself."

"Isn't that the truth? We only enjoy what we let ourselves enjoy." He pulled a gold pocket watch on a chain from the folds of his clothes and flipped open the case. "Well, at this point, I'm going to need a nap. We will have dinner at five o'clock sharp. We'll have some entertainment, some dancing, and a feast to celebrate your arrival."

"I'm sure Shannon will love it."

"Oh, it will be just you and me. The ladies will entertain us."

My glass was halfway to my mouth as he said that. "Excuse me?"

"They will feed her today, take care of all of that. They'll do a ritual juice cleanse meant to honor you. She'll come to you refreshed, pampered, decorated, and maybe a little bit hungry—for you!"

He chuckled.

"I have no doubt you'll be pleased, Marco."

CHAPTER 10

I WAS DIPPED, washed again, drizzled with scented oil worked into my skin, soaked in a soothing chamomile cocoon, and then gently washed and rinsed again. My hair felt silky from the hot oil conditioner. Every pore of my body was wide open and alive, rejuvenated with the oils and masques.

I was given a spice-scented deodorant and helped into a fluffy terrycloth robe. While my hair was blow-dried and curled, my nails and toes were painted a delicious rose color. Once again, oil was sprayed onto my forearms and calves and massaged into my skin. My feet were encrusted in warm cotton slippers while I sat in a chair and watched the hairdresser work her magic.

She was a true master at design. Delicately, she wove strands ribbons of gold into my hair, braiding them, twisting them into patterns coiled around the top of my head. The bulk of my hair was curled and allowed to flow in ringlets then carefully pinned up and adorned with tiny tuberoses and miniature buds that looked like roses. More gold ribbon was used. Several long strands were tightly curled and allowed to hang down my back.

A tiny gold chain with a single ruby was pinned at my crown and allowed to dangle on my forehead. She placed long golden bangles adorned with rubies and other stones on my ears with a matching ring on my right hand.

They applied foundation and began drawing dark black outlines around my eyes, similar to how the other wives wore it. It made my eyes look enormous. My eyelids were garnished in turquoise powder, and my lips were smoothed in a tingling red lipstick.

When she showed me with a hand-held mirror what my profile and back of my head looked like, I nearly didn't recognize that it was me. The bright colors on my face and the glistening jewels dangling at the sides of my neck and on my forehead did make me look like one of them.

A princess.

The robe was removed, and several women brought in armloads of saris. I'd read about how sari fitting could sometimes take hours, that there was an art to it. The older woman's critical eye picked out several, holding them up to my face and neck, bunched them to drape at my hips, and finally selected a half dozen to work with, sending the others back.

She stepped close to me, her finger dipping in a little pot of some kind of pink salve that smelled exotic, infused with flower and spice scents, even a hint of cinnamon. She smiled as she rubbed a small dot into my skin just under my earlobes. Then she pasted over both my nipples with the salve, which stimulated and tickled them. And finally, she came to her knees and applied the mixture to my nether lips, rubbing it into my now-hairless mound, even placing a small dab at my anus, which caused me to jump. Several of the ladies giggled.

As the women started drying off and getting dressed, the woman worked her magic, wrapping the white silk under wrap around my chest, under my arms, and about my waist. With a deep turquoise sari sprinkled with tiny silver threads, she wrapped the fabric over one shoulder and around my chest again, leaving the ends loose, while she used another slightly lighter shade of turquoise sari with a gold border around my waist, bunching it at my left hip and securing it by tying it off with the undergarment. Another paper-thin transparent fabric draped over them all, which she tied in a loose knot at my other hip. She pulled ends of the large panels of fabric, tucked yardage in various places until she was satisfied they wouldn't move.

She asked me to walk a few steps forward, turn, and come back to her, which I did. With her hands together, she bowed her head, adding several strands of delicate gold chain around my neck that hung to below my waist.

Jeweled sandals were carefully placed on my feet. Someone also snapped in place an ankle bracelet of tiny tinkling bells I'd heard earlier and added one at each of my wrists. Bending her forearms at the elbow, she asked me to flash my hands back and forth to make the bracelets come alive.

The enchanting sound was laced with the infusion of the exotic spices.

The women formed a circle, and I was encouraged to follow their movements as they dipped their arms and hands below and then above their heads, twirled, and shook their wrists to make the bells tinkle. They showed me how to cover my face with the light veil, to bow my head, cast my eyes down, and concentrate on the motion of my fingers as we moved gracefully in the circle.

At the end of my little rehearsal, we all bowed to each other with our hands together.

The room exploded into spontaneous chatter as the women piled up all the used towels and repositioned the lounge chairs and pillows. I was handed another smoothie, a yogurt mixture with pomegranate and other blended fruits and given a slice of fresh coconut. Handing me a toothbrush, I brushed my teeth, drank some mint tea, and they applied more red lipstick.

We were ready for the show.

I felt like one of the wives as we made our way down the hallway of statues, our bells tingling, filling the air with wonderful scents. I wasn't the tallest, but one of them. We followed behind the oldest wife, two-by-two. The English-speaking woman whispered in my ear.

"Do not look at him. Make him watch you, but don't make eye contact until you are alone. It is most good for the time later on, if you understand."

Oh, I understood. I knew it would drive Marco crazy. I knew everything about this little caper would send him right over the edge. Way under my skirts, my flesh quivered at the thought.

I couldn't wait to see how hard he'd have to restrain himself.

We entered the great reception area, which contained several couples I presumed to be loyal subjects of the sultan. They followed behind us as we made our way to the banquet hall and throne room. An enormous golden statue of a sitting elephant with four arms sat on a raised dais on the far side of the room. Dwarfed in comparison, an ornate pair of golden chairs sat on a one-step pedestal just below the statue. I saw to my left a large banquet table had been prepared that served only two people. The sultan was on the left, and Marco sat in a black tux on his right. True to my promise, I lowered my eyes and did not look at him.

I followed the other pairs of wives as we circled in front of the giant statue, and one by one, we each bowed our heads, our hands together in prayer and adoration.

I could hear the sultan's deep voice, and his belly laughs. I didn't hear a sound from Marco. Perhaps he hadn't noticed me?

We formed the circle we'd practiced in the bathing room, each of us following along behind the other, making the sweeping hand movements and dips. We shook our wrists and twirled. I pulled the veil across my face, bowed when I was closest to the sultan, like the others did. He whispered something guttural to Marco, and I heard the word enchanting, but I wasn't watching either of their faces. I demurely allowed the veil to cover my face again as the circle turned, and I was presented once more.

Our movement stopped, and we formed one long line, all dozen of us. Out of the corner of my eye, I could see Marco with his legs crossed, elbows on the armchair he was sitting in, with the fingers of his right hand drawn across his face below the nose. There was no question he was breathing heavily, and I took great pleasure in that thought.

But I remained with my eyes averted. I even made eye contact with the young wife who had given me directions and the pregnant one, who both gave me a slight bow and smiled. I was caught off guard as the whole line of women kneeled on one knee, their heads low and palms held together in front of them. I was the last to make the formation, but I waited, just like they did.

The sultan walked down the line, touching each one of his wives, placing a hand under their jaw and raising their eyes to see him. He stopped for a moment in front of me but didn't touch me. Several times, he said something private to the woman. He chose three, including his oldest wife, whom he took by the hand and led down the hallway, through the entrance, and off down another long corridor. I presumed it was the royal chamber, but it was just a guess.

Nobody else moved. I heard Marco approach, and then I saw his black trousers and his polished black shoes. I felt his fingers encircle my right wrist, the tiny bells calling to us, as he commanded me to stand, and I did so. I wasn't sure what to do next, so I kept my eyes cast down until he delicately pushed up my chin, and I could no longer avoid the searing heat from his eyes.

As he led me across the marble floor and up the

wide staircase to the room upstairs, I turned and smiled to the nine other wives who had watched, lovingly bathed, and coached me. They now smiled back.

It was a scene right out of one of my storybooks when I was a child. It was all about the handsome prince choosing his princess above all others, in an unbelievably beautiful old palace on an island kingdom in the middle of the Indian Ocean.

CHAPTER 11

W HEN I WAS a kid, I remembered reading a cowboy
story—in hindsight, it probably was a romance
novel I found of my mom's—about a guy who mail
ordered his bride from China. When she arrived on the
stagecoach, she was dressed in her traditional Chinese
garments and his hands were shaking as he had to peel
away her silky top with the funny buttons made out of
knots.

I probably shouldn't have been reading that book,
since I was about ten or twelve, but I couldn't put it
down. I'd known exactly how he felt because I'd never
held a girl, let alone undressed one with callused hands,
nervous and ill-equipped to know what to do. I'd
imagined her exotic scent, her mannerisms, and the
way she averted her gaze downward. Plus, she was so
tiny the cowboy was worried he'd offend her or, worse
still, somehow break her brittle bones.

Leading Shannon up the stairs in her flowing robes

with her brightly painted face and the music of her little bells at her ankle and wrists made me feel the same way. I was right back to being a young boy with no experience. I had never been shy before, but her beauty overwhelmed me.

Yes, it *overwhelmed* me.

It had been sort of a lark that I put her in the sultan's harem's hands. I didn't think of it as too significant, just a new experience, something she might find fun. But seeing her dressed in the silks, watching her dance and copy the other traditional women who had been trained their whole lives to be what they were today, touched me some place deep. I was delighted with the outcome, but I was ashamed I'd put her through it.

No denying it. I did force her to play this game. I never allowed her to object. I forced my way on her, and for that, I was not proud.

I never wanted to make her do anything like this again, and my shame only grew with the lust I felt for her. This was not the man I truly was. This was not the honorable man I'd become. I was play acting a role that put women as second-class—put Shannon as subservient to me. And she did it. She followed along with something she never would have chosen on her own.

I could feel her eyes on me, wondering why I wasn't saying anything. But I didn't want to further embarrass her in front of a household of people where this was the custom. But it wasn't Shannon's custom. It wasn't the way I wanted to treat the woman I planned to spend the rest of my life with. This discussion had to be done in private where I wouldn't cause her shame nor bring shame on the palace and my very dear friend.

I closed the door behind us as we entered our room. Someone had brought champagne on ice and a huge bouquet of large, colorful wild jungle flowers set in a Chinese urn. The whole room was filled with the heady, flowery aroma.

Shannon stood in front of one of the carved wooden posters on the bed, pulling the sheer silk material from the canopy between her fingers. She knew something was wrong. Her downcast eyes were not due to the part she played. She thought I was displeased with her.

Nothing could be further from the truth.

I walked to her, tipped her chin up, searched her dark eyes, felt the soft porcelain texture of her skin under my thumb, and tasted her ripe red lips. She melted into me, her arms traveling up to my neck, her lips breathless, ravenous, and hungry. I folded her into my chest like the precious doll she was and gently swayed while she squirmed in my arms.

At last, we parted, and she stepped back.

"What is it?"

"I am ashamed, Shannon. That's the truth."

Her scowl was quick, her spine rigid, and her chest heaving, making the tiny golden and silver strands of her clothing twinkle with the rise and fall of her full bosom. "What's happened, Marco? What's changed?"

I was in deep, unchartered waters. I'd been trained to do all kinds of indescribable things, but I suddenly felt myself unable to speak, and the longer it took to respond, the bigger problem I had.

"I had no right to ask you to do this," I whispered, studying my idle fingers.

"*This*? Explain." Her face was hard to read, but it certainly wasn't friendly.

"They've turned you—I made them turn you into a slave girl, a harem girl, someone who is my property, and for that, I am ashamed."

Her anger was quick to flash. With her hands on her hips, she shouted at me, "You son of a bitch." She didn't care if the rest of the palace heard her, either.

Now I was confused. "Shannon, I'm sorry, but let me explain."

"No. Are you so uptight that you don't want to do a little dress up? Did you ever do that when you were little?"

"Yes, but—"

"I'll bet you even tried to get little girls to play doctor with you, too. It's disgusting but kind of normal."

I recalled trying to get some free feels in junior high school under the guise of bumping into one of the early-development girls in my class. I was just as scared in front of them then as I was right now.

"A Halloween costume? Did you ever buy Em or Rebecca some really kinky underwear? Come on, Marco, I know you, goddammit."

"Shannon, please lower your voice. I don't want—"

"Well, at this point, I don't care what you want. I care about what *I* want. I've been pampered in more ways than you can imagine—oiled, shaved, massaged, and other stuff too. I've been fed elixirs to make my womb receptive to your seed. I've even had my butthole waxed and oiled. And all the time this was going on, I was thinking about you, doing it for you. To bring you pleasure. And you're ashamed? You're ashamed I want to be your fantasy princess?"

I'd gotten it all wrong.

Fuck!

"So you tell me? Are you going to participate or are you going to watch me pleasure myself?" She stepped close, her hot nipples brushing against my shirt, her hand with the little bells sliding down to my enormous cock, which swelled as she squeezed me. She looked at my lips as she whispered, "Do you have what it takes to fuck me, Marco? Use me? Hard? To make my whole afternoon worth it? I want you to touch me all over. But mostly, I want you to touch me. Here." She grabbed my hand and placed it against her left breast, right over her beating heart.

And then she kissed me, ramming her tongue down my throat.

I sprang to action. I slipped the sari over her shoulder, exposing her left breast and bit down on her knotted nipple as she moaned. Putting one hand between her legs and the other over her shoulder, I lifted her up and tossed her back on the bed. I watched her writhe in front of me, exposing her leg and her luscious thigh as she undulated her hips forward and backward while I threw off my tux, quickly unzipped my pants, and discarded my shoes, leaving everything in a pile at the foot of the bed. I started to unbutton my shirt but was fumbling so I rolled up my sleeves instead and presented to her my throbbing member as my knees walked their way up to her hips so she could touch me.

One of her hands cupped and squeezed my package while the other unbuttoned my shirt. Her hot tongue was at my belly button as she yanked the shirt back over my shoulders and threw it across the room.

Her curls were falling, becoming unpinned. The little ruby necklace on her forehead was crooked, but she slid underneath me and took me into her mouth, pressing me way down into her throat all the way to my stem.

Her saris were wrapped and tied. I couldn't find a zipper or button anywhere but began to pull at her folds, releasing the material slowly until the turquoise silk unpeeled at her sides. She put my cock between her breasts and squeezed. I picked her up, hands beneath her rib cage, and moved us both back up into the middle of the bed. She tried to keep her knees together, and my fingers soon found out why. Up and down her moist slit, my forefinger felt her velvety petals, completely hairless, until I slipped over her stiff little bud and entered her.

She arched back, giving me access. I spread her knees apart and saw her glistening mound, covered in some exotic salve as I dipped my head and tasted her. She rocked her hips and moaned, pulling at my hair and throwing her knee over my shoulder as she reached for me.

I flicked my tongue back and forth over her petals, sucking their juices, inhaling her sweet womanly goodness. Her fingers stroked and pulled me until I gave in to her need, touching the head against her opening and scooting herself down as I thrust up slowly, but eventually deep.

Back and forth in long strokes, my member glided in and out of her, fully visible, fully open so I could see it all.

I turned her slightly to the side, with her leg and bent knee still over my shoulder, and fucked her at an angle. I kissed her neck, her ears. I dug deep, holding her tummy and stroking her from below while arching up into her. My thumb pressed her nub again as I felt her muscles begin to milk me. She turned onto her belly, holding my fingers in place as her leg slipped over my shoulder. On her front, her fingers buried between her legs.

Coming to my knees, I plunged my tongue into her hot, juicy sex, gently curved her rear up by placing my hand under her belly, and pulled her back and onto my shaft.

Shannon shattered as I lazily stroked and kissed her from behind, my hands roaming over the smooth contours of her butt cheeks, my fingers exploring all the nude parts of her. After a succession of deep, quick lunges, I held myself deep inside her, and then we released together, collapsing on the bed.

Her makeup was smeared, her hair in a wild tangle all over the bed and her shoulders. The ruby necklace was gone, discarded somewhere on the bed. The well of flesh at the top of her shoulder smelled like cinnamon, as did the spot just beneath her ears. Her nipples tasted like ripe berries.

I was still catching my breath as I pulled her up on

top of me and reveled in the smooth swale of her back and how it felt to rub her wet sex over my package. I could feel her heart beating urgently. I lifted her head, pulled her up by the waist, and kissed her.

"Did you feel it there?" I whispered as my hands squeezed and massaged her left breast.

"I did. And you?"

"Everywhere. You were made for me, Shannon. Every little thing about your body belongs right here, in my arms."

She traced my eyebrows and the arch of my ear and my lips, planting tiny kisses there and under my jaw. "What was it like when you saw me? Did you like that I didn't look at you?"

"I didn't like it at all. I wanted to strip you down and fuck your brains out right there in front of everyone. But that wouldn't have honored you or me. It made me insane. I was so filled with lust and couldn't say anything about it, couldn't even show it to you in my eyes. I wanted you to see how you made me feel, watching you dance, watching you shake your little wrist things."

Our fingers mated, resting on the turquoise silk. Her dark eyes searched mine, her hair slung to the side as one of her earrings dangled like ripe fruit.

"What was it like?" I asked, wondering.

She placed her palms on my chest and rested her

chin there. I held the rest of her long body between my thighs, stroking her backside and hip as she spoke.

"They do this for fun. It's just like dress-up when we were little."

"God, I wish I'd grown up with you and played dress-up. I would have played doctor, too."

"See, I told you. I don't understand why you felt—"

"I misunderstood. I really did. I worried that you felt forced, like I'd forced you into something non-consensual, because I remembered you hesitated."

"I did," she nodded. "When they took all my clothes off, I was shy. I covered my chest, but after a while, I got used to their hands on me. I pretended they were your hands. I felt myself becoming softer, more beautiful. I *wanted* to be your gift."

"You are my gift."

"But it's special when someone *wants* to be your gift, your vessel. That's what they call it, becoming a more perfect vessel. For you, Marco."

"Gosh, I got it so wrong."

"I like the play." Her fingers slipped up my neck into my hairline as she arched her way up until our lips touched. She wrapped her legs around my waist and moved her sex against my navel. "Play is fun."

She sat up then slid down to find me, and our eyes locked as we were joined again. I felt every little quarter inch of her channel until I could go no farther, and then she pressed down, inhaled, and I moved another inch inside her.

Her hands against my shoulders, she lifted her torso up and down on me. She looked at me with eyes of need, and as her lids closed in slow motion, she shuddered. "Don't stop. Don't ever stop."

CHAPTER 12

MARCO WANTED TO give me a tour of the palace grounds after breakfast, so we came downstairs and helped ourselves to a lavish platter of cut fresh fruits artfully arranged. Assorted bowls contained foods I'd never eaten before, like a green mint porridge with herbs and coconut milk, black rice pudding, kneer with quinoa, garnished with cinnamon and chickpea crepes with sautéed vegetables, peanuts, and sweet-hot chutney. Everything was colorful and tasty, and I suspected healthy.

Marco went wild for the chutney, covering his fruit generously. We sat down at a large table set for twelve as one of the servants brought us both a chai latte.

"It's past nine, and no one's up," I whispered.

Marco stopped shoveling the fruit and hot mixture down to check the surrounding area, but all we could hear were the sounds of staff working in the kitchen and gardeners outside chattering.

"He's not an early riser." Marco leaned into me and planted a soft kiss on my lips. "I'm kinda surprised you're up so early for the tour. I'm a bit worn out myself." His dreamy eyes set my panties on fire. I blushed. "Lovely," he said and kissed me again.

I realized he wanted to tell me something else but apparently decided against it.

Several loud blue parrots cackled outside in the side garden, making a mess, splashing water everywhere, screeching in and out of the large fountain, and chasing after each other. They left as quickly as they'd arrived. Tall spires of torch ginger and fragrant yellow bush flowers bloomed, sending a sweet floral scent our way, reminding me of jasmine or gardenia. I could almost forget that there was another world out there.

"He lives here alone with the wives?" I whispered. The eeriness of the empty rooms sent a chill up my spine.

"And his children and grandchildren. I believe they are traveling in India at the present time. It can be quite a crowd when they're all home. But you should see it when they do these pilgrimages. They used to book whole floors of hotels wherever they'd go. I remember, some years ago, he went shopping in Paris for some rings and bracelets for some of his favorites, and he walked into Cartier's with a bag of jewels the size of a croquet ball. He gave them a list of what he wanted but let the artisans at Cartier's design everything. He had it delivered by armored courier protected by a small army some months later."

"But there's nobody here. Doesn't he have security?"

"They're here. You saw some of them in front. The compound is fenced and monitored by state-of-the-art stuff. He doesn't want to feel like he lives in a prison, but he takes it seriously. Trust me, he's well-guarded, or I wouldn't have brought you here."

"I would think so. Where does the family live?"

"There's a gated compound on the north shore where some of the grown children and their families live, and it is heavily guarded by palace guards, like the uniformed ones out front, who have served the family going back several generations. They and their families live here as well, which is part of the perks of the job."

"So he cares for everyone, supports everyone?"

"Family who want to stay can stay. Most of the adults leave and go on to do other things. Once that happens, they cannot return. It's his natural attrition, or this island kingdom would be overrun."

It reminded me of an old man I knew once who ran a hotel at the ocean in Oregon. Constant turnover and nobody stayed full time, he'd complained to me. And none of his kids wanted to take over the business, so he just continued on well into his eighties. It filled me with a bit of melancholy.

"If they need surgery or something specialized, where do they go?"

"He has a medical staff who work at a small clinic he built. For anything major, they go to the Maldives, India, or even Europe. As you saw, the island is only forty-five minutes from the Maldives, two hours to the southern coast of India. The world has gotten to be a much smaller place since the days of his grandfather. For many generations, the family was isolated. It was a long trip by boat, before air travel. Now he can reach any big city almost as fast as we can in Florida."

"He must be one of the richest men in the world to be able to support this household."

"It helps when you have claim to an enormous oil field. His grandfather actually went to school in Texas around the turn of the century and made friends in the oil business. He came back, did his homework, and invested in making claims offshore just north of us before anyone else was even exploring there. The area now is known as the third largest oil field in the Indian Ocean. He secured his family's legacy—forever. Arjun's father was a playboy sultan killed in a plane crash during World War II, so he was raised by his grandfather, who forbade his sons from moving off the island or spending too much time being absent landlords, unless they relinquished their inheritance."

"He was a smart man."

"Very. But in many ways, a lonely one. He knows his children—many of them—would rather set up businesses of their own, not just live here, as beautiful as it is. So he's encouraged several to attend college in the U.S. and elsewhere. Several have married and settled outside the tiny kingdom. The two I'm going to be watching over want to be builders. I'm here to protect them."

"He's like the fairy tale, except in reverse. He's the princess who is walled up in her golden kingdom and longs to live outside the beautiful palace. And everyone else wants to get in.

"I actually think he's okay with it. When not with his wives, he spends his time in solitude mostly. He has an enormous library. I'll show it to you sometime."

"Please. Now, with a dozen or more wives, will he take on more?"

"I doubt it. He doesn't travel much any longer, and finding a wife is complicated in the culture here. There are week-long family meetings, events that have to be catered for hundreds of people. The bride price has to be fixed. The parents of the bride pretend the groom is not good enough and hold their daughter for ransom. For a good girl from a good family with no health issues, the whole process can be exhausting, I've been told. And with a stable of beauties at his beck and call, I don't think he feels the need any longer to search for a new one."

We finished our breakfast and a second cup of the

delicious chai. "Well, doesn't appear we'll have company. I'm ready for my tour."

Marco took my hand, and we slipped out a side door from the main pavilion, following a lush garden path. I had brought the sheer sari that I wore last night, using it was a loose shawl over my shoulders since the air was still chilly and not at all humid yet. We came to a huge pool complex—a shallow one next to a much deeper lap pool. In the shallow pool, there were slides for children and water features that popped up at random to spray the whole area and then disappeared. There were tables and lounge chairs scattered about the patio overlooking the blue water. A small dollhouse was decorated with bright inlay tilework and sat in a small forest of ceramic mushrooms of various sizes children could sit on.

Seeing this deserted area where children should be laughing and playing made me a bit sad.

The wet areas were fully gated off, but we pushed through a metal entrance door opening to an area outside the complex. The gate clicked, locking behind us and startling me. Marco held up a key card for re-entry.

We walked past several bungalows tucked in a cluster in the dark foliage. Several of them had golf carts outside the front door or parked in the driveway. We passed a tennis court and an intricately carved open-sided wooden pavilion. Through another gate, we followed a narrow garden trail that turned sandy, spilling out onto a peach bisque-colored sand beach. The color contrasted nicely with light turquoise waves rolling and slamming on the wet sand, as the ocean showed its petticoats in the hissing surf.

Ahead of the waves was the horizon, with no obstruction, the water a slightly darker shade of aqua. Billowy white clouds rose high in the sky, churning and rolling, slowly heading our direction.

I knew India was just beyond that horizon, but as we stood there, hand in hand, I felt like we were in the middle of some undiscovered and abandoned island.

"Are there a lot of these, islands with palaces?"

"Most of them are in ruins today. Mostly uninhabited islands, atolls really. He once told me not all of them were mapped, if you can believe such a thing."

"So who owns them?"

"They mostly align with the country closest to them—Maldives, India, or Sri Lanka. Like everything else in the world, it's shifted as the world-wide balance of power shifts."

I inhaled the moist air, now warming up. It reminded me of a really good day at the Gulf back home. But as far as I could see, there was only ocean, clouds, and sky. "Why would anyone want to leave?" I asked.

"It's because of what's out there, the opportunities we cannot see, the feel and taste of the unknown. Adventure," he whispered, slipping his arm around my waist and kissing the top of my head.

CHAPTER 13

W E WERE WAITING for the house to get up, so I used the time to go online, using my SAT hotspot. I determined that our plane had been diagnosed with an engine problem that would require a new one be installed. It would delay our trip home for nearly a month, so I approved the work order but contracted for another plane to arrive as soon as was possible. They promised it within three days. I thanked Ron for his quick work and for lining up our Plan B checklist.

That new engine was going to leave a fifteen-million-dollar hole in my budget for the year, so I asked for and got terms. Everyone was doing that nowadays, even governments.

Next, I called Harry.

"Hold on, hold on. I'm sorry I wasn't there to meet you at the airport. I'm close, should be there in about an hour."

"Just wondering. I'm not usually the first one to

arrive. Nobody's here, Harry. What the hell's happening?"

"He's in a rather crabby mood these days. Rather anti-social, if you ask me."

"He seemed perfectly fine to me," I objected. "But I mean, nobody's here. Where are the kids? Usually, those bungalows are overflowing with relatives. Is there some plague I haven't been told about?"

"No, Marco. Just the luck of the timing. Are you managing to have a good time? Kind of nice to have more access to him, isn't it?"

"Yes, we've had quite an adventure already. I'll tell you about it later." I hesitated discussing business over the phone, but I wanted him thinking about some of the answers I needed. "Harry, the stuff you sent me from the kids is very light. I mean, there are more gaps than swiss cheese. They are taking this seriously, I hope. It's not like I'm helping them put up a condo complex in Florida, right?"

Harry said something I didn't understand and sighed heavily into the phone.

"Okay, since you're going to find out about it anyhow, Khalil had a little problem with a casino in Macao and wound up blowing a big advance the sultan gave him for the mission. I've actually been working with the casino today, getting a loan for him to get some of it back. Of course, he insists he'll win it back. Considers it a temporary setback."

"How much money did he lose?"

"It—it was a lot. But I managed to get about three quarters of it back, at a competitive interest rate, too. But my dad is not to know about it."

"Don't tell me things like that. If he asks me, I have to tell him. I don't like being put in that position. If he can't know, then don't tell me, okay?"

"Okay, I see your point. No problem. His trust fund can handle the payments. But I've got to let him know tonight his gambling days are over until this project is finished. He's not going to be happy, not that he'll complain to the sultan."

"I should hope not. He really wants to believe in these kids."

"You are wrong there, Marco. He doesn't want them to get killed. He already knows they'll be making mistakes. You're hired to make sure they don't make lethal ones."

"Well, getting in bed with the Macao tribe is not very smart."

"I agree. The Triads are in it for the money, and as long as the money comes, we're all good. Don't worry about this. I think I got it all under control."

I wasn't so sure, and this bothered me more than I would be able to show. Shannon was already listening to my conversation, even though she tried to look like she was reading. I'd piqued her interest.

"So when do they arrive today? The sultan said this afternoon. Do you have any details on this?"

"I think they're en route. Haven't talked to them today. They know you're coming, so they'll be there."

"If they're not rotting in some prison somewhere penniless."

"Look, it's not that bad. You're getting worked up over nothing, Marco. You'll see."

"How's the writing coming?" I decided I'd beaten that dead horse enough and wanted to switch the subject.

"Slow. My time will come. The public isn't ready for a gay Westside Story or Romeo and Jules. See you in a few."

"Ciao." I shook my head in disbelief.

Shannon was studying me. "Is there a problem?"

I wasn't going to lie, but I couldn't tell her everything. "I'm dealing with a couple of young pups fresh out of graduate school. The usual problem is raising capital for this kind of project. Here, we don't have a lack of funds. We have an issue on the budget and line items we're spending it on."

"Do you do that too?"

"When one of the principals is gambling his stake money away? Yes, then it becomes my problem. It's a behavioral issue. They're going to have to become disciplined if this is going to work. I'm going to lay it all out there tonight, or I'm not going to Africa."

"I'm sure you will. I'm sure they'll listen."

I liked her faith in me. I was starting to doubt I'd made a good decision to get involved. But part of me wanted to protect the sultan, too, since there were any number of outfits he could hire who would rip him off and not do a very good job of protecting his kids.

"Thanks. Okay, gotta make a couple more calls."

Karin Atkin picked up the call before it rang on my end. "We're expecting the boys here this afternoon, and I have some questions I'm going to press them on. What else should I add to my laundry list—and thanks for all the reports. Very helpful."

"Thanks, Boss. Not sure if you saw it online, but they've appointed a new Minister of Culture, and he's a missionary-trained Christian. I'm not sure how much influence he has with President Mtoto, but the fact that he's a new hire tells me your president has had some kind of religious conversion or a shakeup in his cabinet, perhaps."

I was trying to think about how that would be a problem.

"Your boys are Hindu, right?"

"They are."

"I'd buy them a couple of gold crosses to wear when they're swaggering around the project and definitely when meeting with any of the political leaders. I know if they were Muslim this would be a sacrilege. Do you think they'll mind?"

"Well, that's a good thing to discuss with them, then."

"And I wouldn't mention the sultan's wives. They generally don't like that, either."

"They probably wouldn't like gambling then," I added, suddenly seeing a path forward in my discussions with the boys tonight.

"Definitely not. Now, if it was in the neighboring valley, then you'd all be wearing prayer beads and covering your head."

"Me? You mean the boys."

"Right. We'll make sure you bring a nice bible with you when you go, just in case."

"A good plan. What else?"

"Well, Forest will probably tell you, but they caught a bunch of Somali pirates who tried to take over a Chinese cargo ship yesterday. He was headed into port here. As expected, nobody lived to tell the tale, but the point is that there are apparently several groups out there trolling the waterways, and we want to be careful. Watch everything. Even check your security at the palace. These guys are getting bold."

I'd seen little crafts rigged with an outboard motor barely the size of the lifeboats on these huge merchant marine ships go after these ships in a pure stupid David and Goliath move. Consequently, the ships started installing water cannons, since they weren't allowed to arm their crew and everyone knew it.

The cargo ships weren't very maneuverable or fast, but they could cut right across a little skiff or blast everyone out of their seats with their hoses. It was a fool's game played by desperate men who were trying to save their loved ones at home being held hostage.

"Thanks for the tip. We'll keep an eye out, and I'll mention it to the sultan."

She handed the phone to Nigel.

"Hey, Boss, tried to get some drone footage when the story first broke, but the air was locked down."

"No, that's not a hill you want to die on. Good thinking. But there are others?"

"Tis the season. Been practicing take-off and landing. Night vision is super defined. These lot have me dancin' a jig."

"Good. Anything else?"

"When are you going to work an invitation to the palace for us? We'd even do dishes for you."

"Maybe when it's all over. I've got some fierce conversations happening tonight, and then I'll drill down on what we need to get us up to par, because this isn't it."

"Righto."

"But Shannon and I are having a good time, managing to stay out of too much trouble."

I found her over near my side of the bed. She'd taken her top off and had wrapped her upper torso and head in the veil that showed everything. She slowly turned, taking the little steps she'd been taught. She'd put her ankle and wrist bracelets back on, and the sounds of the tinkling bells brought back extremely erotic memories.

I lifted the phone back up to my ear. "I'm going to sign off. There's something I have to take care of, and it won't wait."

I hung up and ran to her side, peeled back the veil from her face, and kissed her while my hands slid down to her perfect ass. I whispered in her ear, "So we're playing dress-up, are we?"

"I thought you wouldn't mind. Looks like you brought yourself a stash." She pointed to the open drawer beside the bed. I didn't know what she was talking about, but I'd put her ruby headband and the bells in there this morning when I was cleaning up, just to get them out of the way.

"Oh? I wasn't aware there was anything—" My fingers pawed through various items. Gels and stimulating creams, textured condoms, and several sex toys were lying in the bottom of the drawer with her necklace and the other two bracelets. I put my finger to my lips. "Oh my."

"I didn't know you were into that stuff," she said.

"Well, *I* didn't bring them. I think they were provided."

She picked up a metal tube and read, "Ruby red cherry excitement jelly. Looks like it's even written in Arabic as well."

"It doesn't surprise me." I took the gel from her fingers, unscrewed the top, and sniffed it. "It does smell like cherries."

Her big eyes watched me squeeze a tiny bit out and taste it. Then I fed her some. My lips started to tingle, so I pressed more from the tube onto her lips and kissed her.

"Mmm. Very nice, Shannon."

"Is it for me or for you?"

I took a step forward, our thighs rubbing against each other in a casual movement. I was so hot for her and hoped we'd have enough time to get the party started.

"Here," I said, guiding her to sit on the edge of the bed. "I want to try something."

Her eyes were half-lidded as she leaned back on her elbows, the turquoise silk still wrapped around her perfect skin. I grabbed the zipper at her hip, peeling her pants down to the floor. My hand traveled the full length from her knee, up the side of her thigh, then dipped into the top of her black lace panties. She spread her knees. I slipped the elastic at the inside of her upper leg to the left, exposing her deep pink lips, all puckered, plump and moist already.

I took a long time to squeeze a line of gel on my forefinger about two inches long, set the gel down on the table, and let my forefinger apply the pink goodness up and down, running inside and outside her delicate lips, ending with a gentle press on her clit.

She moaned, her head arching backwards, so I applied two fingers to her channel, pressing her clit again with my thumb. Her flesh was on fire. Her chest grew blotchy with red; her nipples became tight knots.

Her arms reached out to me, whispering, "I want you inside me, Marco. Please."

Taking one of her hands, I placed it on the front of my pants. She worked the buttons until she could take hold of my throbbing member, collected gel from her own sex, rubbed it all over me, and then stroked, fondled, and squeezed.

Stepping out of my pants, I pulled her body closer to the edge of the bed, rubbed my shaft over her needy lips. The tingling sensation grew as the gel began to warm. I watched her guide me and, when she moved her hands to my rear, pulled me inside her. I held her legs up to my chest so I could enter deep.

"Is this what you had in mind as far as dress-up?"

CHAPTER 14

WE WERE INTERRUPTED by a voice coming from downstairs. Our bedroom door was closed, but whomever it was began running up the marble steps—an unmistakable tap-tap-tap of shoes on stone. Marco was riding me from behind, and I was just about to come.

"Oh no!" I moaned into the pillow, knowing he was going to pull out and waste a perfectly good heavily ribbed condom. I scrambled to get decent.

Marco swore under his breath and bent over, holding his package to stop an enormous explosion I was going to sadly miss. We ran into each other naked, looking for our clothes buried in the silk sheets, coverlet, and pillows. He managed to get his boxers on. I was still in my black panties and bra when the bedroom door burst open.

"*Hola! ¿Cómo estás?*" the twenty-something young man said in his blue championship Warriors warmup as he ran straight to the middle, covered his eyes, turned around, and left.

"I'm sorry," apologized the muted voice on the other side of the heavy door. "I thought you were alone, Marco."

"You fuckin' moron. I told you I was bringing Shannon."

He opened the door, the back of his head facing us as I continued to find my clothes. "No. You. Didn't. But it doesn't matter. I should have given you privacy."

I was completely confused. "Who is that guy?"

"That's Harry, the sultan's son and social secretary."

"He's allowed to barge in on you like that?"

He rolled his eyes and shrugged. "It's a long story."

Marco slipped on his slacks and motioned for me to take my clothes into the bathroom to finish. I left the door open so I could hear their conversation.

"Okay, Harry. The coast is clear."

"Hubba-hubba, Marco. You've been working out."

"I *always* work out, and you're an asshole. That's never okay."

"Guilty as charged, but man, look at those pecs."

"I mean it, Harry, you're testing my patience. This was not cool. You violated her space."

I peeked through the crack in the doorway and watched Harry walk over to the bed and examine our little experiments—the little hand-held buzzer, the cherry gel, and two opened packages of pleasure palace extra-large condoms, because we'd used the other one already.

Harry crossed his arms. "No, Marco. You violated *her* space, and from the looks of it, you did it more than once!"

"Shut the fuck up!" Marco erupted.

I thought they were going to come to blows, so without the benefit of a brush, I slipped out the doorway into the room barefoot, disheveled, lipstick smeared, but fully clothed.

"Well, hello, gorgeous," Harry said to me, coming over to take my hand and kiss my knuckles. He toyed with the little bells on my wrist. "Cute."

"Unbelievable," Marco muttered, turning his back to us.

"So this is the lovely Shannon. I totally approve."

I didn't warm to his overly flirtatious expressions, nor did I like the fact that when he talked to Marco, he looked as much at his chest as his eyes. I found Marco's zipper pullover and tossed it over to him, and he immediately slipped it over his head, covering the beautiful abs he'd worked so hard to develop. "Thanks."

Both Harry and I sighed, and then I stopped myself and started picking up the wrappers and straightening the bed.

"I really am sorry, guys. It's been three years since I saw Marco last. He is the favorite of all my sultan's friends. And I'm so happy he's come here to help us out. And if you are a friend of Marco's, we're going to get along just fine."

I wasn't too sure. I just continued straightening the pillows and putting the toys back in the drawer discretely. I sat on the stairs leading to the bed platform and waited until I turned invisible.

Harry sat down where Marco had his computer open, moved his briefcase onto his lap, and pulled out a sheaf of papers. "I brought these things you asked for, copies of agreements and some permissions. The boys have other things, which I hope they'll bring today. Have you seen them yet?"

"No," said Marco, absent-mindedly reviewing the paperwork. "I don't see any permit issued by the Minister of Culture or a declaratory letter, either. Do you know anything about this new hire by the president, a new minister?" He looked up, noticed my sitting in the shadows, and motioned for me to come over to him. He sat, and I climbed onto his lap.

What our visitor couldn't see was that Marco had slipped his fingers down the back of my pants, harmlessly swishing the top of my butt without paying any attention or addressing me. He was listening to Harry prattle on about his half-brothers and how difficult they were being.

"You're making me think perhaps I made a mistake coming here," Marco said. Then he leaned forward and kissed my back, through the fabric of my top, of course.

I was balancing on his thigh, alternating my weight so that it gave me delicious pressure against my nub. He whispered in my ear, "I know what you're doing, and you won't get away with it."

"What?" Harry asked, thinking the comment had been addressed to him.

"Shannon and I were having a conversation earlier about getting dressed up for dinner. Is there someplace we can go for a private dinner one of these evenings?"

"Actually, there's a very good Indian restaurant over by the control tower at the airport. It's in that little strip mall?"

I continued undulating so slowly that Harry wouldn't be able to see it. It didn't take much to register my need against his thigh. I turned to speak to Marco, enabling me to adjust my hot sex, moving it back and forth against him.

"I'm starved," I said.

I looked down at his lips while I licked mine. I grazed my fingers backwards over his cheek and let my forefinger trace his bottom lip while I drilled him with an expression I was glad Harry wouldn't be able to see.

"Me too," he said, his fingers slipping back down the gap in my waistband until he reached the crack and stopped. I planted a long, languid kiss on him.

Harry jumped up. "Okay, I get it. I interrupted something, didn't I?" he said, slipping his briefcase strap over his shoulder, scratching the back of his head. He headed straight for the door, but then I didn't see, I only heard, it open and close, because Marco had started searching for my nipples, his hands sliding up my ribcage.

He picked me up as I straddled him, walking me over to the bed. "You're gonna make me an old man, Shannon. I haven't had this much sex since—" His eyes smiled at me before his lips did. "Since the last time at your place. I'll never forget that night."

"Nor will I."

I shed my clothes, and he removed his pants. I waited for him on my belly while he made some choices from the drawer. "We're out of the condoms, but we have a few other things here we've not tried yet." He held up a brown jar and unscrewed the top and smelled it. "Nice. Cinnamon?"

"They used some wonderful cinnamon massage oil on me yesterday. Let me see." I held my hand out, and he placed the open jar on my palm. "Yes, that's it."

He took it back, dipped his finger in it, sliding his

hand beneath me and traveling from the circular massage of my clit back up all the way past my anus.

"It's a healing salve, I think. It feels wonderful, cool and stimulating."

"I see," he whispered.

He was up to something, so I turned my head. He was twirling something small, a little navy-blue plastic object that looked like a baby's pacifier with a bulb on the end of it.

"What's that?" I asked. My radar began to flash, but my pulse quickened.

"An experiment. A little something new, if you've never seen one."

"What is it?" I asked again.

"Can I show you? If I'm very gentle?" His devilish smile made my insides twist in knots. Without him touching me, I could feel the pulse of my sex, full of anticipation.

I nodded.

He dipped the little bulb end into the jar, twirled it a turn or two, leaned over me as he slid the object from my gaping sex back up towards my anus, and then very slowly pressed the bulb end inside me.

I inhaled at the sensation, the forbidden feeling of something I'd never done before. He was breathing in my ear, asking me if I liked it.

I nodded again, gasping, having a hard time catching my breath. Marco turned the little object, refreshing the salve and sparking the sensations again inside me. He drew a soft green silk pillow underneath my belly, kissed both sides of my butt cheeks, tenderly touched my flesh, and made me shudder, and then he lifted my pelvis up with his hand bracing my belly and inserted himself into my dripping sex.

Very slowly, he stroked me in and out as I nearly exploded with need. He carefully crouched over me, moving his hips back and forth, fondling my lips with his hand beneath me. I felt the spasms beginning, the long, rolling orgasm stronger than I'd ever felt before when he thrust deep, held me firm, and pressed down, sending the plug deeper still.

I moaned my pleasure, and he asked me if I was in any pain, and I answered, "God no!"

He increased the pressure, sliding deeper inside my channel as the little object delivered the dull ache I was beyond grateful to receive. I inhaled, my muscles clamping down on him as he spilled deep and hard.

Several minutes later, he stroked my hair, kissed my cheeks, and whispered again in my ear, "I think we're going to have to go to that little purple shop off Gulf Boulevard when we get home. I can see you're beginning to develop some latent talents and appetites I had no idea you had. I don't intend to let you leave me behind."

"I look forward to the instruction, my love."

I knew the very first night we slept together in Boston during that little gift to myself of one perfect, anonymous evening with him that he was going to be my addiction. I had no idea where it would go or how strong it would become. I knew I'd jump into the fire with him anytime, anyplace. I needed him to teach me how to keep him satisfied and how to explore my own boundaries of pleasure and satisfaction.

And I knew it might consume me.

That's exactly what I wanted.

CHAPTER 15

W E'D BEEN SUMMONED downstairs for drinks before dinner. The servant told me the sultan's two sons were arriving any minute, and there would be a few extra guests for dinner.

"Perfect. May I ask, is this a formal dinner? Should I wear my tux, evening wear?"

"I don't believe so. The brothers have traveled far today. They arrived by boat."

"Really? I didn't know the sultan owned a boat—you mean a yacht, right?"

"Yessir," the young servant said. "But the boat belongs to the brothers."

"I see. Well then, we'll be down in about thirty minutes. Tell the sultan I'm looking forward to it."

"Thank you, sir. I certainly will."

Shannon put the long dress my assistant had picked out back into the padded garment bag and zipped it back up, placing it in the closet. "Makes it simple," she said with a shrug.

I didn't put on a tie, but I liked the look of blue jeans with a long-sleeved button-down shirt as crisp, not too formal, and slightly hip. I wasn't old enough to be their father, but these were mid-twenty-year-olds who had lived a wealthy, spoiled lifestyle and were very experienced travelers. I anticipated our conversation was going to get slightly intense, and I needed their respect, in all ways possible.

Shannon was loving the silk sari and the jewelry. She'd lined her eyes with black. Her cheeks were rosy, and her lips lusciously red. Her hair was pinned up with little rhinestone clips, allowing some strands to drop to her back. She also had on her bells. Every time I heard her walk across the room, I had very naughty thoughts.

"What's so funny?"

I placed a palm at her cheek. "I like this new you."

"It isn't too much?" she asked.

Her dark hair and flawless skin contrasted with the shimmery turquoise material wrapped over her head and around her neck. I pulled one corner away so I could kiss her without interference. "You're so beautiful, Shannon."

She blushed, averting her eyes, and then finally returned my breathless gaze. "Thank you."

We descended the steps to join a small crowd in the

grand room. The sultan wore green robes tonight with a matching headwrap garnished in the front with an enormous emerald. A small white feather extended out of the top. His first wife was on his arm.

I was surprised to see him wearing makeup consisting of heavy eyeliner, face powder, and a touch of lip gloss. His dark eyes greeted me warmly and then studied Shannon before he quickly glanced back to me.

"She is becoming an Indian princess, no?" he whispered.

She was speaking with Harry as he admired her sari and was oblivious of the attention she was getting.

"You have no idea," I said and bowed.

"She is adventurous?" His eyebrows elevated, waiting for my answer.

"More than I thought possible."

"And you've only been here one night. Very exciting. Her spirit embraces the palace with grace and dignity."

"I think if you came to Florida you'd be wearing flip-flops and shorts and a floppy hat, Your Highness."

"You'd transform me into a beach bum?"

"It could be done." I looked around me at the opulence, the beautiful colors of the inlay work and golden trim. It was his cocoon. His safe place. "Shannon tells me the beach heals everything. What would it be like if you walked the surf, ate king crab, and drank beer at sunset, my sultan? Who would you be then? Would your costume make you a different person?"

"Interesting discussion, my friend. Perhaps in another lifetime," he said and winked.

We heard Harry laugh at something Shannon told him. I noticed the sultan's eyes were sad. "Did he bring you the items you requested?"

"I haven't had time to review them thoroughly. I need to have a conversation with your boys this evening. A rather frank one."

"Good. Very good."

"I understand they own a vessel?"

The sultan rolled his eyes. "I made many mistakes as a father, but my biggest one was indulging them too much. You will have to evaluate whether or not they are ready for this project, Marco. It gives me no pleasure in saying this. I am disappointed in their behavior of late."

"Harry—"

"Should keep his mouth shut. We will not speak of it, because I don't know about the gambling debt in Macao."

"I understand."

The sultan's wife approached and slipped her arm inside her husband's. "I see your Shannon is enjoying the saris we fitted her for."

"She does. Hardly takes it off. Almost wants to

sleep in it."

She pulled her hand up to her mouth and giggled, partially hiding it from me. "I am glad you were pleased."

I couldn't look her in the eye. Being pleased didn't even begin to describe how I felt when I first saw her walk into the room yesterday evening.

Asrid, the sultan's wife, was adorned in the same colors as the sultan. Her sari was golden yellow and forest green, covering a deep green silk undergarment. She also wore an intricate gold and emerald necklace and clusters of dangling emeralds for earrings.

A servant appeared, holding a silver tray of glasses of some fruit and a light purple yogurt drink. I was going to drink it in one gulp, but the sultan held his glass out in a toast.

"To a successful business venture."

I could drink to that. The mixture was delicious.

I caught sight of Absalom entering the great room, followed by two other young men about the same age with longer hair. They were craning their necks as they looked up at the dome the columns and stained-glass ceiling above. Absalom stood next to his brother and whispered something.

Studying the two friends of the boys, I didn't like what I saw. It wasn't specific, just some internal radar I had when it came to sizing people up. It was obvious they weren't used to being around such wealth, which meant they traveled in different circles. It could also mean they were aiming to take advantage of the boys. The sultan, if he was concerned, didn't show it.

"Your Highness, I'm going to go re-introduce myself and make sure they leave time to discuss some questions I have."

"Please," he said, gesturing for me to cross in front of him.

I broke up the little foursome, extending my hand to Khalil. "Marco Gambini. Nice to see you both again." I shook Absalom's hand as well. The friends faded back a step and allowed us to talk.

"Hey there, coach," said Khalil, who addressed the two friends. "This guy, Marco Gambini, he's a decorated Navy SEAL. Did all sorts of shit—jumps out of airplanes at night and crap. Really cool stuff."

He didn't sound like the engineering student I was expecting to meet. He'd gotten taller than the last time I saw him. He'd almost lost his Indian accent entirely.

"Navy SEAL, huh? You guys fight in Afghanistan or Pakistan?"

I was aware that people who were from India, regardless of their birthplace or family nationality, were sensitive to the location of our deployments and with whom we were embedded. So I gave a big whiffle ball answer to that one.

"Mostly South America and Africa, man." I made sure my handshake hurt just a little. If there was going to be a man contest, I wanted to win the first round.

"I'm Yassir."

My brain calculated several things and came up with the probability that he was Iranian. Names in this part of the world were very important and were not made up or chosen because they sounded nice.

The other friend didn't come forward.

"Yassir and Hamid found this great catamaran for us. Did Harry tell you?"

"He did not," I lied. "Where did you get it?"

"Male."

"Shannon and I were just there. We could have met up with you, but your father said you were in Mumbai."

"Yes. We had some business things to handle. There is a Nigerian Department of Trade in Mumbai. We went there to get our permits. They said it would take about five days to get all the signatures. So we did some traveling," said Khalil. "Went back and they still weren't ready, so we flew to Male on our way home and met these two gentlemen. It was pure luck. They were helping a British couple sell their boat, so we bought it."

"You bought it from the couple from the U.K?"

"They were very ill and had to sell their boat. They

had to go home, but their agent sold it to us. Very good price."

I was afraid to ask.

"Does your dad know?"

"Yes, yes, I believe Harry told him about it tonight. We are going to take the family out tomorrow for a little demonstration. It's really cool, even sleeps fourteen, and we have a crew we've contracted with. Now we will be traveling in style."

"Where?"

"I beg your pardon?"

"Where will you be traveling to?"

"Oh, all around here, the Maldives, Sri Lanka, maybe take it up along the East Coast of India."

"He doesn't like our idea, man," muttered Absalom, who had been pretty quiet.

"Oh stop. You don't know that." To me, Khalil said, "Wait till you see her. She purrs like a kitten. A big, white kitten."

The waters in the Indian Ocean were well known for piracy. The thought of two twenty-somethings worth several billion between them cruising around pirate-infested waters would give me nightmares if I was their father. And their use of this boat was dependent on the crew they'd hired, so everything was out of their control. Literally everything.

But I had to deal with first things first.

"Khalil, you've managed to do a lot since I first agreed to sign on to work your security in Nigeria. I have to ask you, is that still a priority for you?"

"Oh absolutely." He turned to Absalom, who nodded enthusiastically.

"What about all your permits?"

"Still waiting. We paid an extra tax to get it pushed up the line. Nigeria is very, very busy. Very prosperous. People coming from all over the world to help them build sustainable infrastructure."

"Housing. You're building housing."

"Sure, sure. We build it the green way."

"Did you have to promise it would be green? I'm just not sure you can get all the materials there. You'll have to look into what it all will cost."

"Well, we have you, right? How much does it cost to build a house then, Marco? A two-bedroom house, small size. Green. You tell me."

"First of all, it depends on where."

"Of course. Different building standards for flood zones, etc. Like here. Monsoon windows. Danger of flooding here in really bad storms since our elevation is only four."

"Four what?"

"Four feet. From sea level."

"Oh, now I understand. Yes, those things factor into your building costs. But before we go there, I want to make sure it's feasible, and they'll actually let you build. You have to get the permissions, Khalil."

"I told you, Khalil," Absalom interrupted. "Mr. Gambini, we appreciate everything you're doing for us. Maybe you could get the permits for us. Rattle their cages a bit?"

"In Mumbai?"

"Yes, exactly."

My patience was waning. The whole project was beginning to look like someone's wet dream, and not the kinds of dreams I'd been having lately, either.

"You need a project manager. Someone to do those types of errands. But that person has to know what the rules are, first. I'm hired to do something else. I'm supposed to create your security plan. To keep you safe. And—" I was beginning to see boogie men behind every column. I also didn't want to appear too nega- tive. "We can talk about all that tomorrow. Tonight, I need to go over with you exactly what you do have, who you've talked to. We may have to make some calls tomorrow."

"Sure, we can do that."

I exhaled, relieved. They were going to let me look at all of their files—I didn't pick up any resistance. But there were some huge blind spots we had to shed light on first.

The timing of our talk had been perfect. We were

called to take a seat at the table. As we made our way to the dining alcove, I was going to break away and follow Shannon to the dinner. But Yassir mumbled to the side of Absalom's face, "Hey, can you get me a seat next to that Indian chick over there? The pretty one."

My forward movement stopped all of a sudden, and someone behind me ran into my back. I grabbed an arm off both Absalom and Yassir, yanking them out of line and over to the corner.

"Shannon's with me. She is engaged to me, and if you value your life, you'll be polite, and stay away. Do you understand?"

Yassir's forehead wrinkled as his eyes widened. With new appreciation for who I was, he said, "Oh, my bad. My bad."

I was going to forgive him for just being a clueless dickwad until he added, "But way to go, Gramps."

CHAPTER 16

MARCO SAID VERY little during dinner. I did small things to entice him, which didn't warrant a smile, nod, or any reaction. I began to feel he might be annoyed with me. Harry and I had become great friends during the evening, and I invited him to come down to Florida and visit since his permanent address was Brooklyn with his mother.

Perhaps something happened when he spoke to the boys.

Or when he spoke with the sultan?

I didn't have the room for any of the items presented on silver trays loaded with sweets and delicacies brought out for dessert. I did take a chai latte.

Even the touch of my thigh against his didn't elicit a reaction. With my elbow on the table, I balanced my head on the palm of my hand, turned, and spoke to him, trying to keep it just between us, barely moving my lips.

"Everything alright?"

"Um hum," he answered, nodding.

"Are you sure?"

That's when he looked at me, smiled, and whispered back, "You worry too much. I've got a lot on my mind. That's all."

So it did have to do with the brothers!

I noticed he'd been focusing on the two strangers sitting at the end of the table next to Khalil and Absalom's mother. She was relaxed when speaking with her sons and reserved when speaking to the others. But that was the custom.

A couple we had met during one of our walks sat near us. They had come to ask the sultan permission to marry, since she was one of his daughters. They were young, barely in their twenties, and had met in their first year of college in New York. He was of Indian descent, also a Hindu, but had been raised in the states.

"Did you get permission?" I whispered the question.

"He has to offer the bride price to my parents first, which signifies his acceptance. If they approve, then we can wed," the young man said.

"Will they negotiate much?"

She answered back, bobbing her head from side to side, "This is just a formality. We've already decided we'll be married. But we're attempting to satisfy the traditional values of our parents."

They still looked so young. When I was her age, I hadn't yet let a man, boy, anyone touch me or even kiss me. That door was closed, and I wasn't even motivated to explore what I might be missing.

Because I was so much younger than Marco, I wondered if he saw me as being young, like the sultan's daughter appeared to me. I thought about all the beautiful women he must have slept with during his years after Em and before Rebecca. All the women who had tried to throw themselves at him when he was a SEAL. With his dark hair and onyx eyes, ripped body trained to perfection, I bet he was beating women away every day.

But I did have one advantage. I had fallen in love with him, maybe not as I loved him now as a full-grown woman, but to the fullest capacity of my twelve-year-old heart, because he was kind to me, and Em had told me all the stories. I felt as though I was with them on all their dates, even felt the tension between them when they decided to wait to marry until after he came back from his first deployment. Em returned to college after the break, and I didn't even get to go shopping for her wedding dress. He was overseas, and Em was hit by that drunk driver, killing her and her sorority sisters.

He'd looked so handsome in his white uniform. I pretended he came back to town not for my sister's funeral but to see me. I had a hard time forgiving myself for those thoughts because I achingly missed my sister, my confidant, the one who should have had the happily ever after I was now going to have.

I heard the sultan's daughter whisper to her fiancé, "I don't think she's listening."

"I'm sorry. You reminded me of someone. I sort of had a daydream there for a second."

"That's okay. It's getting late. I think we're going to turn in," she said. "If you feel like it, come to the baths tonight. I promised I'd meet my mother there and spend a little time. You're welcome to join us. It will be very low-key. A good soak in the scented pool will help you sleep better."

"You know, that sanctuary is how I imagined Heaven to look and feel like," I answered.

Her fiancé leaned across the table and whispered, with his finger crossing his lips, "Shhh. I'm not supposed to know anything about that room, since we are not married."

"Someday, after they take hold of your fiancée to prepare her for your wedding night, you'll hear all about it. It's really quite miraculous. I know it's not fair, but I promise you the wait is worth it."

I caught the sultan watching me. His smile was gentle. I genuinely liked the man.

"Let me see what Marco will be up to, and if he's

tied up, maybe I'll take you up on your offer."

They got up, said their good-byes, and left. Several others left as well, leaving the sultan alone at the end of the table, so I rose, asking him if I could keep him company.

"Of course, my dear. Here, finish my pear. I can't eat it."

"I have no place to put it, but thanks," I said as I sat perpendicular to him.

"Things are going okay with your handsome Marco?"

"Yes. And thank you for all of this. I'm not sure what I was expecting, but your generosity in sharing your family and your beautiful house with us is most appreciated."

He smiled, placed his hand on mine. "Tell me about your father. He must love you very much."

A sharp jolt of sadness rippled over me. I took a deep breath and began.

"He was closer to my sister, and when she passed, he never quite got over it. So my relationship was a bit fractured, but we tried. We've gotten as close as we can be at this point. He really drilled Marco about bringing me here, worried that it might be dangerous. Having adventures and taking risks are scary to him. And I'm all he's got left."

"He should be very relieved to know that you are

marrying someone who knows how to take care of you and keep you safe. I wish I could have Marco stay here with me and protect my family. But your father is very lucky. To have a man, a true warrior, to love and care for his daughter, it must make him feel very grateful and relieved."

"I never thought about that. I'm going to tell him what you said."

"Don't tell Marco. His head will get—big!" He stretched his arms to show how large his head could swell.

"I meant my dad. You put it so beautifully.

"Let me ask you something. When your wedding day comes, would you consider perhaps having it here in the palace?"

"I couldn't ask you to do that."

"Of course not. That would be rude. But I'm offering."

"Let me discuss it with Marco first, and if he says yes, then I'd be delighted." But concerns and thoughts of the expense it would cause my friends was a factor, too.

"Your parents, of course, would be my guests here, as well."

"They'd be pinching themselves for a week."

"Ah, here is your handsome fiancé now."

Marco placed his hand on my shoulder and spoke

to the sultan. "I'm going to go see if we can iron some things out tonight, so we're going to meet over at Khalil's bungalow."

"Very well. Good."

Marco leaned down and kissed me on the cheek. "Not sure how late I'll be, so don't wait up for me, okay?"

"No problem. I've been invited to wander over to the baths for a soak. I don't think after that I could wait up for you, so take your time."

Marco shook the sultan's hand and once again kissed me on the check.

I WALKED ALONE down the tiled passageway with the golden domes and carved archways. I had just come from a room with a roaring fireplace in the center, heading to another warm and moist room full of scent, steam, and relaxation. But the breezeway between where I was walking, with its little openings in patterns above the intricate tilework, was chilly. I wrapped the sari around my shoulders tight, lifted the delicate fabric at the back of my neck, and pulled it up over my head while continuing on toward the scented chamber.

I pushed open the metal gate and found several of his wives there, some lounging on chairs and several others in the pool, which is where I was headed.

I slipped my clothes off, folding them with the

beautiful sari on top, placed my shoes under the padded lounge chair, readjusted several pins in my hair to keep more of my hair from falling into the water, approached the lip of the pool, and then stepped in.

Today, white petals floated in the turquoise blue water. A wooden bucket with natural sponges floating in a scented mixture was placed next to me. I took to washing off my arms, then sat on the edge, washed my legs, and slipped back into the pool.

The warm water was soothing, and as I sat down on the ledge under water, I still felt the swelling of some of my delicate body parts, reminding me of my all-too brief last encounter with Marco this afternoon. I heard his whisper in my ear, his hot breath making my pulse quicken, the way his big hand gently held my belly against him, my back feeling the solid wall of his chest.

The sultan was right. I was lucky to have him in my life. If I could give back a fraction of what he was giving me, I'd risk it all to do so.

CHAPTER 17

"**K**HALIL, I CAN'T authorize your new friends to come with us to Africa. I don't know them. They're not properly vetted."

He shrugged, not upset by my refusal of his request.

"All I said was that I'd ask. He probably knows this."

Absalom was checking his cell phone, finally tossing it on the table in front of him. I knew he wouldn't have any service.

"We gotta get Dad to install a tower. Someone would pay for it," he mumbled to his brother.

I couldn't believe I was seeing this. I concentrated on being clear, calm. I put my hands together, resting my forearms on my knees, and began.

"I'm not sure we're ready for this project right now, guys. I'm not sensing there is the focus, the discipline we need to pull this off."

Absalom frowned. Khalil's eyes flashed anger.

"What do you mean? Marco, you've been paid a lot of money, brought here, and—"

"And I'm doing my job, Khalil. He's hired me to protect you both, not build houses and get you both killed. You're out there running off to Macao, buying boats, and partying like you were in college. That just isn't going to cut it, nor will it instill any confidence in my team or the team we want to hire. Maybe you better think about it and get back with me tomorrow, okay?"

"Yeah, but at this point, we're the ones who have done all the work," Khalil shot back at me.

"Not true. I've flown a team over here, three of them doing research as we speak from the Maldives. We don't have a valid set of permissions—don't get me wrong, we have a ton of paperwork, but not the kind of paperwork that will get you the green light you need. You bring new people into the mix and bring them *here* to your father's house. You've just spent—what?— a million dollars on a boat?"

"Nine hundred and eighty-six," Absalom corrected me. "It was a bargain."

I could see I wasn't getting anywhere with them. "Are you sure this couple from the U.K. were the real owners? Did you do a title check and have the hull numbers verified? Could this boat be stolen? Ask yourselves, who are these people? You're smart; you've both done incredibly well in school. You earned that. But what's happening here?"

Khalil's eyes were cloudy. I read defiance in them. "Can't you allow us a little leash to celebrate? In the scheme of things, the cost of the boat isn't that much. A fraction of what we'll spend. But this, this will be fun for the whole family. We can take the whole family out—well, some of the family out. We can go fishing, take Dad fishing. He hasn't ever done that."

I was thinking that there were some abandoned piers in Florida he could go fish at for a lot less than a million dollars. "Fishing is free in Florida."

I knew right away it was a mistake to say that. This time, Absalom reacted, standing in front of me and pointing down with such disrespect, I decided right then and there this was not for me. I'd even decided to try to return the money, all of it, to the sultan before the kid started flapping his gums.

"You don't understand what it's like. This is *our* project, not *yours*, and not our dad's. We bought the boat with our *own* money—"

"You could have hired a first-class project manager to fly over and get your permits. You could have spread that money around and got you some cooperation. You had lots of choices. I'm telling you straight. By the way,"—I stood up too—"don't ever point your finger at me like that again, because I'm not on your payroll. I'm not one of your subjects. You're not the sultan yet. I've just contracted to buy a fourteen-million-dollar engine for my plane, and I have to pay a guy his full salary to wait a month here while it's being replaced. For fourteen million, I could have bought a boat, a brand new pretty nice one and gone gambling. But I didn't do that. I waited here for you guys to show up. And now you're not giving me the time of day."

I began to leave the house.

"Marco, don't!" Khalil shouted after me.

I inhaled, worked on calming myself down so I wouldn't say anything else I'd regret. I was already worried about the report the sultan was going to get. I tried one more time. "What I'm saying is that there isn't anything wrong with streaking off on your own, having a little fun, or having a life adventure. I get it. I did that too. But your choices are all f—messed up. You're making poor decisions. You're not using the talent brought here for you, the full opportunity your father has provided. You're not questioning yourself enough. Anyone can go out there and make a splash and be able to afford to pay for your mistakes. It isn't about that. If you're going to build an empire—again, that's if you really want to do it—and if you want to build something that will last like your grandfather and father have done to preserve your family's legacy, you have to be smart about it and use the advice and knowledge available to you. Otherwise, this beautiful kingdom, this island dating back to the 1100s? You can destroy it in one generation if you're not smart."

I turned on my heel, hoping I'd remembered to give it to them straight, and took off. I ran through the garden. Torches had been lit along the path. The exotic flower aroma annoyed me. Even the casual way the sultan treated his wives and children, giving them free reign to walk all over him and spend ungodly sums of money while knowing they were ill-equipped to handle the project he'd asked me to watch over annoyed me. Was I part of his expendable world too?

Had I fallen this far when I had all the warning signs that this was a trap? Perhaps. Flypaper, something shiny and exciting to share with Shannon. In truth, I'd dumbed down my normally very good radar system, made allowances I shouldn't have made. The spiral of my own bad decisions was eating me alive. Had I mistakenly placed Shannon in harm's way because my own fucking ego was too overly confident this could be my ticket out of my other horrible decisions?

It was Rebecca times ten. I hated that thought. I'd just allowed my own blindness—the very thing I lectured the boys about. I didn't heed the warning signs and ask for help, real help—too proud that I might lose half of my own kingdom. Now I could lose it all.

Instinct told me I should get Paul on the phone and have him bring Little Bird over here and take Shannon home to Florida right away. Like tomorrow morning. I could live with all the talk, let Senator Campbell think I'd lost my nerve, that all my best days were behind me. Had I squandered my good creds? My opportunities?

Maybe that was what made me so angry.

And I hadn't done anything as stupid as fly off to some casino kingdom and lose a couple planes worth of cash. Or buy a boat I couldn't operate by myself. My idea of a real boat was something low and fast. No fucking cupholders and fancy radar. Something built for streaking across the Gulf of Mexico so fast it might propel me forever into the stratosphere all the way to the moon. Something that gave me some serious G's and pulled my cheeks up over my teeth like dropping from thirteen thousand feet.

I had some of those demons. That's why I was so good at finding them in others. Maybe even attracting those types to me.

The hallways were quiet and totally abandoned. The great room was put back together—pillows readjusted and the feast cleared. Gentle trade winds blew the silks covering opened windows around like the ghosts of the sultan's ancestors. I traveled through and around them, climbed the marble stairway, and stopped at our bedroom door.

I had a big problem. I was suddenly re-thinking everything. I was pushing Shannon to do things perhaps she wasn't ready for. Her soft, gentle nature was pleasing and so enjoyable, but she was dressing up. We were play acting about something. She was doing these things to please me, and I had no right to watch her supplicate herself to me. Maybe it was more honest with Rebecca, a bitch I could never fully relax around, someone I could fuck but be worried she'd have a knife to my neck the next minute. I saw all that when I married her, didn't I? She was the opposite of Em.

I placed my forehead against the door.

I've been unfaithful to you, Em. I was tempted, and I caved. I'm so sorry.

I sat on the tiled floor, my back against the door. Bringing my knees to my chest, I lowered my head and let the tears fall.

Tears I should have shed long ago.

CHAPTER 18

I WOKE UP with a headache then discovered the drapes had been left open all night long, so the bright morning sun was pouring into the room.

And Marco wasn't there.

I listened for sounds of the shower running, but all was quiet. Slipping on my silk robe, I slowly opened the heavy wooden door, checking the hallway in both directions and then moving over to the railing overlooking the downstairs.

I heard noises coming from the kitchen, but there was no one seated at the long table we used last night. No one used the pillows and chairs in the great hall. Through a window next to the front entrance, I saw one red-suited guard standing against one of the massive carved wooden columns with another seated on a settee next to him.

I turned, leading the way to the throne room, since I didn't think I'd find Marco in the women's wing.

Incense had been lit. A set of bowls of fruit were arranged on a wooden table in front of the massive golden elephant statue, along with several red votive candles. But no one was anywhere.

My stomach began to turn into knots as my apprehension grew, and my mouth became parched. I re-cinched up my robe, turned, and was about to leave the tall room when I heard something. Someone was snoring.

I walked back to the host table and then peered behind it. On the floor were Marco's shoes, next to his bare feet. He was asleep on several cushions he'd removed from the great hall, his jacked over his shoulders for warmth. I knelt beside him, placing my hand on his shoulder.

He flinched, quickly opened his eyes, and sat up, shaking his head. I saw a nearly empty whiskey bottle tucked under a short stool.

"What are you doing?" I asked.

As I leaned over to extend my hand, he got up, slipped on his jacket, straightened his hair, and adjusted his pants. Finally, he looked down on me as he helped me to stand. His normally sparkling eyes were dull and filled with worry and pain.

I could see he wanted to say something, but I was suddenly afraid of hearing whatever he was going to utter.

"What is it, Marco? What's wrong?"

"I'm going to take you back to Florida. We're leaving this morning."

"What?"

He was avoiding eye contact again.

"That's it? You're not going to explain to me why you're here, sleeping in the throne room, still drunk from a bender? This isn't you, Marco. What's going on?"

"I've been doing a lot of thinking. I told the boys last night I wasn't going to take the job. I'm going to give the money back. This isn't for me. A lot of things are going to have to change, Shannon. I've been just going in the wrong direction with both my business and my life, and I have to fix it. I've probably ruined an old friendship, but I won't be responsible for this thing in Africa under these circumstances. I can't take his money. I have to get back to my real life. Not this—this fairytale with you."

He didn't even try to give me any softness, an ounce of kindness or consideration. His cold eyes showed me a calculating focus that scared me. I never thought I could stare back into his face and not feel any love coming from him. No affection. It was like he was looking at wallpaper.

I wasn't going to let him see me cry, but the hurt and pain I felt was nearly too much to bear. But my iron will took over, and I wanted to reflect back to him what he was giving me. Things were sorting in my head as I began to question our last interactions, wondering if I'd crossed some line, offended him some way.

And then anger began to boil up inside me.

How dare you?

Had he used me all this time and finally had enough? Was this the real Marco, the one Em didn't live long enough to discover? I was so glad she didn't. If he could flip that switch inside his head so quickly like this, perhaps he was even dangerous.

I stepped back. Then I took another step and a third, looking at the full length of his body, from his shoes all the way up to the top of his head. He was a statue. A marble, inanimate statue set in some alcove in a Pink Palace somewhere off in this fairytale kingdom.

That's the part that hurt the most. He actually said that. "Fairytale." It had been the place I'd been dreaming and dancing in for the past two days, imagining all the possibilities, all the adventures we could share. But it was fiction. Pure fiction.

I was just the tragic heroine in some play that was over. The costumes were put away, the sets removed. The audience was gone. Lights were out.

It was over.

I turned around and ran down the beautiful, tiled floor, past the shiny turquoise-and-gold infused columns, underneath the carved wooden arabesque-styled pointed archways, under the bright flowers of the most beautiful stained-glass ceiling I'd ever seen. I ran up the white marble steps, pushed through the door that was ajar, and threw myself on the bed.

Here, I could finally cry.

But my eyes were dry. I couldn't shed a tear. The pain was still there. I'd been betrayed, used, and discarded. I'd been dumb enough to fall for all of it. Who was I to expect that this magic and fantasy world had anything to do with me or anything I'd ever wanted? I hated all of it. I sat up, scanning the room. I hated it all.

I quickly dressed and packed my bag. I even left the turquoise sari neatly folded on the bed. I moved the jewelry I'd been wearing last night into the drawer on Marco's side, the drawer that had all those ridiculous toys. The bells. The buzzer. That awful navy blue thing I would never tell anyone about! I was ashamed of how blind I had been.

I didn't want to look at it so slammed the drawer closed.

Then I heard the door open behind me.

"Shannon, I'm sorry. I should explain. That was very unthinking of me."

I whirled around and faced him. "Unthinking? Is that it? How about unfeeling? How about trying at least to let me down gracefully? You used me, Marco. You used my body, which is one thing, but you used my heart."

I ran to him, about to slap him across the face. But I did add, with all the anger I could muster, in a deep, growling, ugly voice. "You even used my memories of Emily."

He saw my hand flinch.

"Go ahead. I deserve it."

"I won't give you the pleasure."

I really hated him now. He was a complete monster. So selfish, dancing around the world like he owned it, like he was the sultan of his own fictional kingdom, pulling strings, using his connections to make people dance around him like puppets. Master manipulator. He pretended to be concerned about making me perform for him.

Oh. My. God.

"So you've packed."

"You said we were leaving today. I'll just wait right here until you tell me we're ready to go. And no, I don't need anything, thanks for not asking."

I pretended to be interested in the book I'd been reading, opening it and crossing my legs in my favorite pair of sloppy jeans. When I got to Florida, I'd cut them up and maybe send them to him. I didn't want to have anything that belonged or reminded me of him.

He knelt in front of my chair. "I am truly sorry. I didn't do this right. I didn't think it through. Shannon, I'm in survival mode here."

"*You're* in survival mode? Think of how I feel. I'll bet those conversations with the sultan were interesting when I was getting all plucked and pampered for you. You two must have had a big laugh. And then you tried to tell me how you were so concerned about how I felt, when all the time you were crafting a creative time to—to—do things to me. Make me wear a butt plug. Abase myself."

He snickered, and this time I did slap him. His head fell to the side. I could see he was totally caught off guard. I was going to do it again when he grabbed my wrist in midair.

"Don't."

I gave him my nastiest stare, reaching all the way down to the soles of my feet I had to dig so hard.

"I understand how you feel. I am truly sorry. But it was not like that for me. I thought—I thought that…" He let go of my wrist.

"You honestly thought you loved me?"

He looked up at me and nodded. "I'm not the man you thought I was."

"I got the message, Marco. No worries there."

"But what I mean to say is that I'm sorry for leading you on with all this. You're right. I think I did take advantage of you. I was trying to—to reconcile the two parts of me. I thought I'd found that part of me that died when Emily did."

His eyes were moist. Mine were bone dry. I wanted to feel sorry for him. I tried to feel sorry for him. But I repeated over and over again in my head that he was just setting me up to use me again.

"Well, I chalk it up to my lack of experience on all levels."

His eyebrow rose.

"If I'd had more experience with men, I might have recognized more red flags. But no, you picked a girl who fell with reckless abandon for you. For everything. I believed all your bullshit, Marco. You picked someone who wouldn't know she was being had. That's the part that hurts the most. Because I don't think I'll ever love anyone as much as I thought I loved you. No other man in the world will ever have that, because my heart just cannot afford it."

My lower lip quivered, and I looked away as tears spilled down my cheeks. His hand cupped my chin, and a finger smoothed away my tears.

"So what was that ruse in Boston? When you dressed up and picked me up in the bar downstairs, for the express purpose of seducing me? Don't you think you used me as well?"

"It's not the same."

"But you started it. You wanted a piece of me. You went after it. You grabbed the brass ring, Shannon. You went bold. You played for keeps. At first, when you told me, I was angry. All the old voices screamed at me about not being able to trust women—and I questioned my judgement. But then the more I thought about it, you gave me exactly what I'd been looking for. You gave me that little piece of you that jumps in with both feet. I wanted some of that. You helped me throw caution to the winds. And maybe I didn't think about the consequences."

"You're actually quite charming. In fact, you're the most charming man I've ever met. Afterall, I fell in love with you when I was twelve and thought about you—"

"You stalked me. Admit it, Shannon."

"I don't see it that way."

"Of course you don't. This might surprise you. I think you're stronger than I am. You're fearless."

"More of your jeweled tongue elixir." I did feel a softening in my belly. I was a hopeless moth to the flame.

"I owe you this much honesty. I love everything about you, Shannon. I even loved that you seduced me. You nailed me. You really did. You hit the bull's-eye. I love how excited you get, and I forget that life isn't a fairytale, because around you I start believing in fantasies and happily ever after, and then I make stupid decisions. I start making decisions from here," he touched his chest, "instead of here." He pointed to his temple.

"I don't want to live with a man who doesn't make his decisions about love from his heart, Marco. A man who only thinks and doesn't feel, doesn't trust himself to let love take over his whole life, is not someone I want to spend a life with. I thought you were that man, that incredible combination of heart and action. You even calculated that picnic at the beach, had it all planned out like your missions. I like that kind of thinking and planning. Because it's what keeps us alive. Gives us something to live for. It's not all about bank accounts after successful missions. It's about what everything else is *after* that's important, Marco. We work hard so we can love harder. It has to be that way for me. And, regardless of whatever else I said, I'm not ashamed of that. I embrace it. The funny thing is you *taught* me that."

"I did?" His fingers played with the hair on the top of my head.

I looked up at him. "I saw it in *you*, Marco. You *are* that man, if you want to be. You're brave and honorable. You'd rather suffer than cause someone else to pay the price, and you knock yourself out at the knees. You really do. You have to trust your heart, because I honestly believe it is the *best* part of you."

"I am a complete fool."

"You told me that already. You even did it on camera, remember?"

He nodded.

"Did I lose you, Shannon?"

I shrugged. "I don't know. You tried to send me away. I packed my bags, but I'm still here."

"What do I need to do to get you to stay?"

"I think you know."

"I have to trust my heart."

"Yes. And?"

He knelt down and took my hands in his. "I want you to stay. You're the best thing in my life. Can you trust *me*?

"It's a practice, Marco. We train, we practice, right? We get better. We get stronger. We build. We don't tear down. And we never, ever run away."

He kissed my fingers. I drew strength from his handsome face, leaned forward, and kissed him.

"No more wrecking balls to my fairytale castle."

"Yes, ma'am."

"So are we leaving?"

"I didn't call anyone yet. But I do have to tell the sultan they're not ready. It would be a huge danger to themselves and everyone else if they went forward."

"Maybe in time then?"

"I'm going to return the money he gave me."

"He'll be disappointed. What are you going to do if he tries to talk you into it?"

"It doesn't change the facts. When they're ready, I'll be there for them and for him."

"I think he'll like that honesty, Marco."

"I'm going to talk to him now. You stay here for a few minutes?"

"Take as much time as you need. He's been a good friend. I understand that."

But before he could open the bedroom door, the sultan burst in. All the color had drained from his face.

"Marco! I'm sorry, but they have taken them. They have taken my boys."

CHAPTER 19

T HE SULTAN GAVE me the ransom note he was delivered.

"Who brought this to you?"

"Korem, one of the palace guards. He said a young boy delivered it on a bicycle."

Shannon was at my elbow, reading over my shoulder. "Ten million dollars. Wow."

"The money is not a problem. I have dollars. Curious that they would know that."

"Do your boys know that?"

"Yes, but they do not know how much I have here. And how do I know my boys are safe? How will they return them? They tell us where to leave the money, but they don't say where the boys will be."

The sultan looked small and helpless. His normally confident demeanor was completely shattered. I wanted to tell him the truth, but I didn't think I needed to put him through that much pain. I'd learned that, in most places in this part of the world, the hostages were often killed right after pictures were taken or a message was recorded. They would just bog them down, since, as slaves, the boys would be useless. And that was the best part of it. They wouldn't be trafficked. But their chances of survival were slim, if I was playing the odds.

"You need to sit down." I helped him to the chair Shannon had been sitting in. "Did you know those men who came with your sons last night?" I was kicking myself for not insisting I talk with him before he retired.

"No, but I knew what they were doing with the boat and everything. People tell me things."

"I understand. But have you ever seen these two men before? Or does anyone in the islands know them by chance?"

"No. I don't think they knew them until recently. But I'm sure, and it sounds like you agree, they are involved."

"Absolutely sure. No doubt in my mind. I wish I'd said something to you last night."

"They normally are not so foolish."

I couldn't believe he was telling me this. "You're making excuses. Now I want you to think about this. Is there anyone in your household here you don't completely trust? Anybody new to the staff?"

"I don't think so, no."

"They were going to take everyone out on the boat today. Do you know where it is?"

"There's a long pier and a deep-water port north-west from here. We use it for receiving things by ship from the islands, India, and Sri Lanka. Absalom told me we would leave from there." He put his head in his hands. "Oh, my god. I'm being punished for all my past deeds."

"No, Your Highness. It does no good to say that. It's not true."

"I should have been more careful."

"Now you're beginning to sound like me."

Harry flew in the door, skidding on the smooth tiled floor as he tried to stop.

"Papa! I just heard. They have left you a note?"

"Here." I gave it to Harry.

"But this is written in English. Why did they not write in Hindi? And they misspelled ransom. You see? They wrote it with an e at the end. Your sons would not make that mistake, my sultan. They are very well educated."

I hadn't noticed that. But then, my spelling wasn't known for being perfect.

Harry went back to keeping up the ruse about not being the sultan's son, probably for Shannon's benefit.

I was concerned about the sultan's blood pressure, and in light of what I knew of his current state of health, he couldn't handle too much stress.

"Can I borrow your car and go look?"

"I'll get a landscaper's truck," Harry said. "That way we can cut across the gardens instead of taking the road. I'll meet you outside the front door." He dashed off to find the vehicle.

"I think you'd be more comfortable if you sat in the grand room and put your feet up."

"I want to retire to my bedroom. I am useless. But I can get you the money. I keep it there."

There were two attendants waiting for him outside our door. They helped him downstairs to accompany him to his chambers. As I dialed Paul's number, I noticed Shannon was in shock. "I'm going to see if I can get the helicopter over here. Maybe have the team come help us find them."

"That's right. You have drones."

I nodded.

"Paul? Say, Paul, we've had an emergency here. The sultan's two sons have been kidnapped and are being held for random. I need you to bring Little Bird over, if you can."

"That's most distressing news. You know they caught a group of pirates, the Navy did just two days ago. It was all over the news today. Just found out about it. They were smuggling in arms from Iran."

"Well, the Navy might be interested in these guys

too. There's a boat involved. I'm going to go see if it's still here. They may be using it to run something."

"You have the numbers? I can have one of your guys look it up."

"Unfortunately not. But I'm calling them next."

"I'm going to top her off, and then I'll be there in an hour or less."

"I'll have them meet you at the strip."

Next call was to the team. Karin said she'd search for reports of missing boats to see if we could get a hull number or registration I.D. She said she'd also give our contact at Diego Garcia a heads-up. They were dropping everything to head to the airport.

I heard a tiny engine outside.

"It's him. What do you need, Marco?" Shannon asked.

"Maybe you could get the keys for the first bungalow, see if anything they left behind tells us something. You know where it is?"

"Yes, but how do I get a key?"

"Let's go downstairs and talk to Harry about it."

We flew down the marble steps and outside. Harry was waiting in a green three-wheeled truck with a dump bed on the back covered by a rounded corrugated metal roof.

"Harry, do you have a SAT phone?"

He held his up.

"Let me dial my number. I want to leave mine with Shannon."

I coded in my phone number, and it rang. I handed it to Shannon.

"Do you have keys to the boys' room at the bungalows?"

Harry dug into his pockets and produced a single key. "Don't tell anyone, but it opens all of them."

I transferred it to her palm. "Thanks, sweetie."

I gave her a kiss and hopped in the little truck. Harry called out for one of the guards to climb in the back, which was a good idea, since I didn't bring my Sig. Harry floored the pedal, but the thing was about as responsive as a bumper car, especially with the three of us on board.

We barreled down the main path in front of the entrance, followed the curve to the right, through a small intersection of connecting paths, and then crossed a fragrant garden with several cascading water fountains competing for attention in the middle. I had yet to see this part of the palace grounds. A team of gardeners was trimming a flowered hedge. Harry waved to them as he cruised by at top speed.

"Is this the fountain they talk about in the note?"

"That one, Ganesh, in the middle."

We quickly zipped passed it.

"We're almost there," Harry barked over the sound

of the diesel motor.

I was concerned about losing the element of surprise with the noisy truck, but speed was also important. I could feel the moisture and taste the salty air, so expected to see the blue waters of the Indian Ocean any second. The foliage separated, revealing a long boathouse on stilts and concrete blocks. Like everything else on the island, it was adorned with carved wooden beams along the roof line, extending over the double-door entrance where the beam curved up and was adorned with a carved creature like that of a figurehead on a ship.

Harry pointed to the odd building. "The goddess of the island lives here."

"Isn't it for boats?"

"It's for her boat. We store it inside. Sometimes offerings are left there by the wives."

"So she is special to only them?"

"She is the goddess of the island. Every island has one. They pray to her. And to Ganesh."

Harry abruptly stopped. A long wooden pier extended easily fifty feet or more out into a perfectly flat and lapis blue ocean. There were no clouds in the sky today. There was no sign of land.

And there was no boat.

CHAPTER 20

I WAS CLOSE to the entrance to the baths as I continued down the corridor, heading towards the bungalows. I could hear wailing and the quick urgent chatter of women who were in duress. Their voices and sad sobbing echoed off the walls.

My heart ached for the mother of the two sons.

Unlike my family when there was a crisis, they were isolated and had only themselves to console. My family huddled together. Stayed tight. Maybe it was too tight because, after a while, I couldn't breathe. My parent's grief was so huge I carried it for years as my silent cross. Maybe this was a better way.

But it was still sad.

I assumed the women would be the last to get any news and resigned themselves to helping the mother relieve her stress in an attempt to help deal with their own. I also knew that those mothers of children who were on the pilgrimage were probably just as worried.

With no real power, all they had was their community.

The early afternoon air was getting hot and sticky. Within a couple of hours, the Tradewinds would start blowing across the island from the east, and things had a chance of cooling down.

Marco told me the brothers were staying in the first house, so I inserted the key and turned the front doorknob but found the door unlocked. I stepped inside to a scene of total chaos.

Cushions were ripped apart, sliced with a sharp knife, and stuffing removed. They'd destroyed every single one, including the tops of several silk-covered ottomans. All the sheets had been removed from the bedrooms and piled up on the floor. The foam mattresses were sliced, hanging over their box springs. Clothes were thrown from the hanging closet, and all the drawers in each bedroom's dresser were upended, the contents spread everywhere.

I searched through the discarded items but was at a loss as to what I was looking for. Anything of written material was prepared in Hindi character fonts, so notes, tickets, and wrappers were useless to me.

But I did find a brochure of a yacht sales office in Mumbai with several boats circled. The prices didn't correlate to anything I could understand, but when I was reviewing the pages inside the brochure, a business card fell at my feet.

Kenny Singh.

He sounded like a salesman. Perhaps Harry or Marco would be able to get information from him that would help. It did give us an idea what they had been looking at in Mumbai, at least.

I carefully gathered papers spread close to the brochure, including several meal and lodging receipts, placing everything in a plastic bag from the kitchen.

As I scanned the mess, I wondered what the thieves had been looking for. It was odd that the pillows would be sliced up if they were looking for cash.

As I opened the front door, I almost missed a pile of papers that had been in a side table drawer, now upended on the floor. Poking out from the bottom of the pile was a cell phone. I used a dishtowel from the kitchen and, without touching it with my hands, wrapped the phone in it and added it to the contents of the plastic bag.

I turned and scanned the living room one more time and then locked the door behind me. I beat myself up about not using a piece of towel before touching the doorknob. But what was done was done, and I was at least bringing something to the group that hopefully would lead to some clues.

On the way back, I hesitated at the hallway, hearing the women's voices on the other side of the doors at the end of their wing.

Should I go see them? Would I make it worse?

Deciding being helpful was the better choice, I opened the gate, traveled the short distance to the entrance of the bath area, and walked inside.

Their mother was on a settee, surrounded by several other wives. She looked exhausted. But others were actively sobbing, wringing their hands and pulling their hair. The older wife searched my face for some sort of news I, unfortunately, didn't have to give her.

She looked at the plastic bag, so I showed her the brochure, and I unwrapped the cell phone, which she quickly grabbed.

So much for preserving prints.

She lit the screen, pressed buttons, and read characters and texts I couldn't decipher.

"Is this your son's?" I asked.

She nodded. The young wife who spoke English approached. "Can I help?"

"Ask her if she can look at the last calls and if she recognizes any of them."

I waited for my answer, and unfortunately, it was no.

"Whose phone is it?"

I heard Absalom's name quite distinctly.

"Can she make the last pictures come up?"

The mother was having a hard time getting pictures to display. One of the other wives helped her out. So now we had two extra sets of prints to deal with.

All of a sudden, the women got excited, pointing to the pictures. She held the screen up to me and displayed a beautifully clear picture of a sparkling white craft with the two boys standing in front of it. I also noticed that numbers on the hull of the ship were easy to read. I knew Marco would be pleased.

"One more favor, please," I asked the woman who spoke English. "The password. She knows the password for this phone. Can I have it?"

The answer was, "July seventh. But spell out the numbers."

I put my hands together as they handed the phone back. "Thank you," I said as I bowed and ran with my plastic bag of goodies, anxious to show them what I'd found.

When the SAT phone rang, it surprised me. I'd stuck it in my back jeans pocket and totally forgot I had it. "Hello?"

"We're back. The boat is gone. Did you find anything or are you still looking?"

"I did better than that. The place was trashed, but I found Absalom's phone, and he'd taken a picture of the boat. You can read the numbers on the front, just like you talked about."

"Super. Where are you now?"

"Almost to the great room."

"I'll meet you there. Harry's gone to pick up my team from the heliport. I was going to go, but I think I'll stay behind and look over those pictures. Good job, Shannon."

"See you in five."

As I entered the great hall again, I heard a vehicle leave the driveway in front. Marco greeted me before I made it to the large dining table. I handed him my bag of booty.

"What's all this?"

"The phone's in there, but I found a brochure from Mumbai. They were looking at boats there, too, and there's a card. And I just picked up everything around it, in case I got anything else of value. I can't read most of this stuff."

He picked up the cell phone and tried to get the screen to light up.

"You have to hit oh seven, oh seven. I got it from his mother."

He dialed as directed and called up the picture of the boat. "I'll be damned. Where did you find this?"

"On the floor. They'd made so much of a mess it got covered up."

"Look at this, Shannon." He enlarged the picture, and I recognized one of the men they'd brought to the house standing at a distance in profile, talking on his cell phone. He was completely unaware he'd been caught on camera.

"Wow. I didn't see that."

"And we have a timestamp when the picture was taken, depending on the setting. But we know when that call was made, and we know who made it. That's some good forensic evidence."

Within minutes of the team arriving, the entire table was taken up with laptops, phone chargers, a fax/printer, and several other electronic boxes I didn't have a clue what they were used for.

The big drone case with the sleek, white beauty and its parts took over several colorful silk pillows of two ottomans pushed together. Nigel was sitting nearby, admiring it like it was his new baby. And I guessed it was.

"Pretty bird."

"She is," Nigel said, running his hand down her body as if he was caressing a woman's thigh.

Karin shouted out, "Marco, we have a hit on the boat. Our friendlies know all about it. A couple from Florida owned it, and it was reported missing a week ago."

"Where are they now, back in Florida?" he asked.

She shook her head. "Presumed dead."

Marco looked at Paul. "Can we find them? They can't be too far away. How fast does this thing go?" he asked his pilot.

"About thirty, thirty-five miles an hour. They've been gone an hour plus, so they could be 40 plus miles away. I don't think there's anything within that range they could moor. My guess is they're headed to Male. That's about eighty miles." He lowered his voice considerably, almost whispering, "Little Bird is faster."

"Karin, let the Navy know where we think they're headed. And see if you can get hold of that yacht salesman. Paul, let's go see if we can get eyes on them."

Forest stopped him. "Hold on there. These guys are hostages, if they're still alive. You go flying overhead, and you've just tipped them off. They have the boat. They'd want the money. I'm guessing ten million is worth the risk to come back. But they won't come back for it with this boat if they think they're being tracked. My guess? They'll dump the kids in the ocean and get a bird to bring them back here for the pickup tomorrow."

Paul let out a string of choice words. Marco was thinking. He finally added, "I know we'll catch that boat. I want to get the kids alive."

"So maybe we take Little Bird. If we think we see them, I'll send out the drone," said Nigel. "We'll get pictures and send them along to the friendlies. But at least we'll know if they're still alive."

"If they're on deck," said Marco.

"Yup, if they're on deck."

It was a sobering thought for everyone.

I had an idea. "Well then, we just have to get lucky. No other way to be sure. And, if we don't try, we'll never know. You lose one hundred percent of the at-bats you don't take. Didn't Joe DiMaggio say that or something?" I scrunched up my nose, not sure if I'd added anything or not.

"Marco, if you don't marry that girl, I'm going to," said Nigel. He wrapped his arm around my shoulder.

As if Marco could get jealous.

But he was back. Marco was back. He looked at me the way he did when I was all dressed up, dancing in front of him with the other wives. It wasn't his eyes I noticed, because I was only seeing him out of the sides of mine. It was the way he cocked his head, the way his chest rose and fell, his fingers rubbing against each other.

It made me love being the object of his desire. I stretched my arms longer, tilted my head in a graceful angle, shook the little bells at my wrists, and let him hear the swoosh of my thighs against the silk layers of fabric.

I was turning his night into magic. It was *real* magic.

For both of us.

CHAPTER 21

I INVITED SHANNON to come along, after checking with Karin and Forest to make sure they didn't need additional help. Harry wanted to stay behind and check on his dad, so we borrowed his van for the short trip to the heliport.

She was more familiar with the routine this time, even managed to get herself strapped in and was the first one other than Paul to get her headset on. I sat up front next to Paul. Shannon sat behind the pilot and Nigel behind me. I asked him to check her seatbelt, and she stuck her tongue out at me.

"She's locked and loaded," Nigel told me with a wink.

Behind them, the drone case had been placed and then opened for quick use. Nigel kept the controller box on his lap the whole time.

"Everyone ready?" Paul asked.

I gave my thumbs-up, as did Shannon. Nigel nodded, and Paul directed Little Bird to climb straight up and then lowered the nose, and we took off in a large arc over the ocean. He flipped a switch, and we had some Star Wars theme songs to fly by. I settled back, since there wasn't much but ocean to look at. A handful of small islands no larger than my car back home popped up here and there. Nigel used his binoculars and called it for no evidence of the catamaran.

I knew the lighter the water the shallower it was, so I figured it would be easy to spot the boat if they'd sunk it. The more we encountered these shallow spots, the more relieved I became.

"Do you want to swing back and forth here, check everything out, or do you want the pictures for the Navy?" Paul asked.

"I want to find the boat first. I want to give the frogs as much information as possible so they can nab these guys in time."

Several bright white sailboat masts were scattered all over the area, but our big boat hadn't been spotted yet.

"Should I turn my drone on? It will register the other boats and store the data. But we won't get pictures until she's in the air."

"I don't have room up here in the cockpit. Any way you can go into the rear seat and turn it on there?"

"No, Marco. Just the nose. I got it right here." He

handed me the black plastic cone no bigger than a bar of soap. "It's registering, so just point it straight ahead and try not to move too much."

"Easy for you to say."

"It will keep us from getting false flags."

"Gotcha. Is this okay?"

Nigel leaned toward Shannon, trying to get a visual of my arm. "Just a second. Let me get out my slide rule."

Paul cackled.

"So you come up here and hold your arm out for an hour, thank you very much."

My SAT phone rang.

"Oh shit. Can you reach it?" I leaned forward to allow Shannon or Nigel space to get the phone from my rear pocket.

There was no mistaking the feel of Shannon's hand pulling the phone out but also giving me a nice little rub. She held it to her ear.

"Okay, just a sec," she said. "Karin wanted to tell you the salesman in Mumbai tried to sell the boys a new yacht, but they wanted to keep looking for a used one. Coincidentally, he just got a call today from a party who thinks he wants to sell his. He was asking about prices and things. He doesn't think it's a real seller call. He's kicking the tires."

"Okay, good. Tell her to have him let us know if he hears from that seller again or if he gets wind of a used

44 Cat Aquila, especially if it has Florida registration numbers."

"She said she would do. Should I hold the phone?"

"Yes, please."

I heard a beeping noise. I focused on the horizon to see if I could find anything and couldn't.

"Yup, that's a sighting all right. It's bigger than a sailboat," Nigel said.

"Hand me the binoculars." I spotted her right away. There were more than two people on the deck, but I couldn't tell who they were.

"I think I'd better cool it. The wind is going towards them, so they'll hear us long before they'll see us. But I can call in coordinates, rough ones. If you want."

"Let's get the bird out there first, Paul," Nigel requested. I nodded agreement and handed the nosecone back to him. He handed the comm to Shannon and scrambled to the rear. A short time later, I heard several clicking sounds. Paul banked Little Bird, retreated a few hundred feet, and began to hover low over the water so we would have a lesser chance of being heard.

Nigel sat back down, strapped in, reached behind him to retrieve the drone, holding it in his left hand, and flipped the on-switch. We heard a low, purring whir of the motor kicking in to gear. With his right hand, he slid open the cabin door, transferred the bird over, extended his arm outside the cabin so the wings wouldn't get caught on the doorway, and just dropped it. He didn't bother closing the door until he was able to take back the controller and start to direct its flight.

Then he closed the door and clicked it shut.

"Paul, you're gonna want to get some elevation or I'll lose signal. We're stretching the boundaries here."

Little Bird did a slow spiral upwards, and after a couple hundred feet, he leveled out.

"That's fine. We're getting some good picture quality. Hold on. There!"

I turned around and saw the white deck of the fat little boat, but when Nigel magnified the picture, we could practically see what kind of beer they were drinking. There were three people on the deck, and as we all studied the pictures, none of them looked like either of the two sons. We did recognize one of the houseguests, though. That was welcome information.

Nigel directed the drone to come back toward us and then take another pass. He skillfully got a good shot of the below-decks, where an open door showed one of three bedrooms on the boat. Someone was hog-tied, wrists and ankles together, lying on their side on the bed. There was just one.

Only one.

But there could be more in the other two bed-rooms.

Nigel took about twenty still photos, which would be uploaded to his computer back at the island. All of them would have their coordinates, as well as the date and time recorded on each of the frames.

"You have enough?"

"Can we get Karin to get into your computer to forward them on?" I asked.

"Sure thing. I have no secrets," said Nigel. "Why don't you dial Karin and hold the phone up to me. I don't want to put this thing away if I have to re-photograph anything."

Nigel gave Karin access to his computer, and about a minute later, she got confirmation that the photos arrived intact. "Karin, make sure to tell them their direction, and that they're traveling about thirty to thirty-five miles per hour, okay?"

I heard her answer back that a cutter was on its way over, and there would be an intercept within the hour.

"Music to my ears, Karin. Looks like we got them just in time. Tell them thanks. I'm out."

She confirmed.

"Hot damn. That was close, but I think we got it done. Now up to the Navy. Thank God for Uncle Sam."

"Good deal," said Nigel. "I'm putting her to bed."

"Does she follow us home?" Shannon asked.

"Nope, you'll see." He handed the comm to Shannon temporarily. "Don't touch that," he said, pointing to the stick.

Unstrapping, he lifted the black memory foam that held the drone parts and pulled out a folded one-foot square piece of netting, attached to a metal arm which telescoped to make it longer. Nigel opened the door again, shouting Paul instructions.

"I don't want the drone to hit Little Bird, and it's dangerous, this part. So I want you to just try to pull up, walk alongside of her on your right. Try to get as close as you can but be the higher bird. This arm expands to about ten feet. But the net is what will catch her."

Paul trailed behind the drone, and above, then slowly lowered us and got us closer. I was praying for no turbulence. That drone could foul our blades, and we'd be dropping to the sea in no time.

But his skillful maneuvering got us so close that Nigel plucked the drone right out of the sky like fishing for salmon. He barked to Shannon to cut the power on the comm. We all breathed a sigh of relief when he carefully maneuvered the netting and drone inside and set it behind us.

"Let's take her home, Paul. I think we got a mission accomplished here. I got a date with a shower. I'm soaking wet."

I chanced a backward glance at Shannon's face and saw her downcast eyes. But then she raised them and smile at me.

I was going to enjoy that shower.

CHAPTER 22

JUST BEFORE WE arrived back at the palace, Karin called us to say that five hijackers had been captured, with no significant injury, and both the brothers had been rescued. We were all in a buoyant mood when we landed.

Harry was waiting for us at the front door. His face was downcast.

Marco grabbed me around the waist and gave him the good news about the boys.

"Couldn't come at a better time. The sultan's having a rough afternoon. He's been coughing non-stop. I saw a little blood on his Kleenex, and then he denied it. Is he sick, Marco?"

"I can't answer that. But it's hard to diagnose when he won't go to the doctor. You get him in for some tests."

"I will. I'm going to stay over a bit until he's feeling better. He worked himself up pretty good."

"That's the way he is. You should know that by now."

"I certainly do."

"I need to talk to him about his plans for Africa. I don't want to bring up too many things at once, so you tell me if he's well enough to perhaps receive some bad news."

"Oh dear. Someone got hurt. They cut off one of the boy's ears?"

I had a hard time keeping a straight face. "Should we go see him and give him the good news ourselves?" I added, "Maybe then we could assess how he's feeling, and Marco could talk to him but just a little bit. Would that work?"

"He won't really tell me. Maybe he'll be more honest with you. I know he has a good heart and just wants to protect me. But, at the same time, this is a complicated family unit. There are a lot of people to consider here."

"Let me see what I can do," Marco said. "Oh, and do I have permission to put the team up here tonight?"

"I don't see why not. They've earned it. I have three vacant bungalows so, if they double up, should be enough private space for them. We'll have a feast tonight to celebrate the return of my brothers. I'll have to get more staff in, but it's easy to do."

"And you promise to get everyone to hold over?"

"Yes, Boss."

"Why, Harry, are you angling for a job?" I asked him.

"I have one, as you know. But I plan parties and events all the time in Brooklyn. For something like tonight, I'm all over it."

"I'm counting on you," Marco said.

On our way to the front door, I posed an idea. "Marco, you should consider hiring Harry. Seriously."

"I have an assistant. But maybe going forward. For our grand opening, whenever that will be."

"You'll get there. I like his energy."

"I do too. In fact, I have another idea as well."

"Tell me."

"I don't want to spoil it. But come with me to speak with him."

We received a warm welcome from Karin and Forest.

"How did you know you'd need the drone?" Forest asked.

"It was just the strength of the team. I don't think we'll do any project without them now."

We headed off toward the sultan's rooms when I remembered the party tonight. "Marco, you didn't tell them about the dinner."

"Thank you. Going to fix that right now." He turned around and shouted out to the two of them.

"And everyone stays over tonight. We have a big dinner, debriefing. Mini board meeting with alcohol."

"I'm up with that," said Karin.

"Tomorrow, we'll get you guys back to the Maldives."

"Cool, Boss! Thanks," said Forest.

I was struck with how the palace was beginning to feel like a fancy office building. The whole place was transforming.

We entered the sultan's chambers, passing by the throne room with his elephant god dominating everything in there. I recognized his younger, pregnant wife waiting by the door.

"How is he?" Marco asked.

"He just seems to want to rest."

"That's probably what he needs," I offered.

"Harry thought I could—"

We heard the sultan's voice from across the room. "Marco, is that you? Please come in."

She moved aside, whispering, "Not too long. He's very weak."

"I bring good news, Your Highness," Marco started off. "The boys have been found, and the U.S. Navy gets all the credit. They might be home in time for dinner. They're going to have to give statements first, and then they'll be home."

"I'm delighted with this. I've been dreading the

outcome. I'll have to get up and make more of an effort—"

But the sultan fell back, disoriented and confused. "The mind is willing, but the body tells me I have to rest. I was looking forward to fishing with both of you."

"We'll do that. We'll do that soon."

"Shannon, you come over here to the other side and sit with me a while."

I did as instructed.

"You sit, too, Marco. Now tell me, Surya says you slept in the throne room last night, Marco. And you brought alcohol in there. Was there something that went on between the two of you?"

"I wanted to talk to you about it."

"Oh, dear. Something else has happened?"

"I'm just going to be brutally honest with you, Your Highness. They aren't ready. Your sons are young in their business years. They understand business theory, but not how to go about getting things done. It's a lack of maturity. It's not a character flaw; they just haven't had to, well, work. They don't understand the concept."

"But they both went to—"

"Yes, very gifted students. That's *theory*. They have no street smarts."

"So what does this mean?"

"We should do the project when they get some experience. I suggest give them something to build here, not this African complex. And here's another thing. West Africa is having problems right now. It's even more dangerous than before. That alone was almost enough for me to recommend we not do this."

"Right now or are you turning me down forever, Marco? Just be honest with me. I consider you—you're a son to me. Please be honest."

"No, I'm not turning you down. But I don't want to be responsible if something happened to them. This whole thing today—it's mostly their fault. They invited those men into your house, Your Highness. You don't have nearly enough security here. You trust everyone and have a big heart. You are extremely vulnerable. They are the same way. They learned it from you."

"So this is also about me? You don't think I've raised my sons to be worthy citizens?"

Marco leaned over and grabbed the sultan's hand. "No, my friend. Hear what I'm saying. Nothing could be further from the truth. They're naïve. They buy a boat without checking the title and spent nearly a million dollars on it, too. That's a lot of money."

"Well, to me, I'd just rather they be happy. If they waste it on things like this boat, it won't really hurt me or them."

"But a million dollars is a lot of money to a lot of bad guys. People do bad things for far less. It bothers me that you are so exposed."

"I do not want to live in a prison."

"You have to protect your legacy. I told them the same last night. If they're not careful, they could undo what ten centuries of your ancestors created here. This little jewel, someone could try to grab it. And they could do it in one generation."

"What's the point of having wealth if you have to be locked up with it?"

Marco looked over to me. I could see he was asking for my help.

"I think what Marco is trying to tell you is that the world is changing. This little kingdom was well insulated from all the rest of the world's problems. Now, you're less than three hours from active wars, concentration camps, and food shortages. There's instability. You can't ignore this any longer. You used to be able to. And it isn't anything you did. It's what's going on out there. Outside."

"I never made demands of the outside. And my family, if they wanted to stay, they could stay forever. I'm seeing that the younger generation want to go live their lives away from this island. I used to think my grandfather was too harsh to not allow us to travel abroad to go to school. Now I understand why. Is my little kingdom dying? Is this what you mean?"

"It will die if you don't change. Who in this family

can run this household like you can?" Marco asked.

"I see your point. So if you're not leaving me and not turning down the job, then what are you saying?"

"I'm saying they aren't ready *now*. I said I'd do it, but not when the odds are stacked against us. Maybe in a few years. They're not ready today."

"Well, that's a problem, then, isn't it? I don't have a few years. I have a year at best, Marco. And not a word of this to Harry, either. You do not have my permission to tell anyone."

"Understood."

"Marco, how did you do it? What special quality made you so successful? Was it your training? You were one of a handful. What made you so different?"

"I was tested, you're right. And some of my colleagues in class expected to and didn't make it. Eighty-seven percent didn't. But the honest truth is that I just didn't quit. I had no options. I didn't grow up in a hothouse where everything was provided for me. I got to experience the value of my own work. In giving them everything they want with no consequences, you not only endanger you and your wives but you endanger them."

"So teach them. Mentor them."

"I made it because I had a huge advantage."

"What was that?"

"I started from zero, and I wanted it with my whole

heart. I was constantly on the lookout for something that would derail me, send me back to the dorms, or make me drop out. After a while, I knew they couldn't get rid of me."

"So what can we do, then?"

"We hire lots of mentors. We exhaust them with information. We make them study things they didn't learn in their programs. We hire project managers and financial managers. We take on less ambitious projects, like drilling wells for villages. Things that don't pay well. We do it because we want to learn and change. They have to study to live in the world, while doing good things that we are proud of."

"Like build houses."

"Yes, that's a good goal. But we don't do this in such dangerous places, not when they're learning. I still think your Africa project has merit. But it's not something we can just do overnight."

"Where will these mentors teach them? Do they go back to school?"

"Well, I'm just now thinking about this, and I'm not sure why I didn't come up with it before. Maybe, Your Highness, they start by working for me first. I have a project on the Gulf. They could help me get that one off the ground. But I warn you, they'll work hard. Otherwise, they'll be fired."

The sultan started laughing and then coughing.

"That would be something, wouldn't it? You? Ordering my sons around?"

"It's not about ordering them around. It's about teaching them to work. Because it's worth it to preserve your legacy. Their legacy. If they care about that, they'll learn everything they need. They'll be unstoppable. A force for good, not some ornament hanging on a fence or in a museum somewhere. Your kingdom will not only survive. It will thrive."

"Let's do it. Let's get this started."

I was proud of Marco for telling him not what he wanted to hear but what he needed to hear.

"There are two conditions, Your Highness," Marco added.

"Go on."

"First, they have to say they want it. I'll work out a plan and schedule, a long-term plan for the Africa project too."

"Otherwise, they don't get to participate. They get fired," the sultan guessed.

"Exactly."

"And the other condition?"

"You give me a couple of weeks, and we'll live in my house. You'll wear shorts and flip flops. We'll go fishing every day. Nobody will know who you are. You'll learn how to cook, bake bread, and go shopping. You become curious about how average people live and cope with their daily lives. You can only bring one wife, because those are our laws. But you come and learn what it is like to live outside your cocoon, in my world. I want to take your training wheels off. If you do it, just for two weeks, I think they will too."

"What do you think, Shannon?" the sultan asked.

"It's the chance of a lifetime, Your Highness. I'd take it."

"The question is what do you think, Your Highness? Do *you* want it?"

"I think I'd like to try when I feel stronger. Not too long, but I should get to the doctor, don't you think?"

"An excellent start. Now you have a short-term goal. Your goal is to get as healthy as you can so you can do well at boot camp."

He fell back in the pillows, laughing and mumbling, "Boot Camp." He coughed. "I'm going to be a fuckin' Navy SEAL."

CHAPTER 23

S HANNON WASN'T ABLE to keep up with me as I took the marble steps two at a time.

"We're going to work on that too."

Her eyes got as big as saucers. "Not me. I'm not a marathoner. I run on the beach a little bit, but no, I don't do running up and down stairs."

"We'll see about that." I finished the steps, looking forward to the shower, and heard her mumbling. And yes, she also picked up a little swearing, placing it in there nicely, just like the sultan did.

She entered the room and sat down, breathing heavy. "Are you going to be one of those?" she asked.

"Our first board meeting is tonight. I'm going to introduce the boys and you as well. Let's see what happens."

"Did you just offer me a job?"

"I did."

"They call it a presumptive close. You just used a

sales skill on me. Your fiancée."

I knew she was going to continue on with the lecture about sales closes. I could name just about every one, including some of the more obscure ones. I conducted a little experiment, trying out another close. I ripped off my shirt and kicked off my shoes.

She stopped talking. Lesson learned. She wasn't gasping for air any longer, either. "Oh? Did you want to go before me? I can wait."

"This is so not fair," she mumbled.

I approached, hesitating to take the final step. "You're not going to slap me, are you? Because—"

"Would you please shut up?" And then softer, she said, "And kiss me."

I reached for her head, my fingers deep in her hair, messing it all up as I preferred it. My mouth covered hers, and I pressed her lips open with my tongue, a full-scale frontal assault. I even felt her knees cave a bit. She leaned against me slightly. I wouldn't let up until I transferred my attentions to nibble her earlobe and then kissed around her neck and down between her breasts.

She was still leaning against me when I was done.

I could see she was puzzled. She was evaluating my performance, perhaps? I decided to wait until she was ready to tell me.

"What's gotten into you?"

"I've kissed you before, Shannon. So what*ever* do you mean?"

"This, this way you're being. That look on your face."

I turned around and looked at myself in the bathroom mirror.

"I don't see it. May I undress you so we can discuss this in the shower?"

She squinted, but I recognized some play acting there. Fake anger.

"Well?" I slid my pants down to my ankles. My particular body part was very happy to see her, bobbing up and down and trying to get her attention.

I unbuttoned her jeans, and they dropped to the floor. She stepped out of them. I removed her panties and top. She wasn't wearing a bra.

"Come, my dear." I tugged at her hand, and she followed me into the shower enclosure.

"What I meant was you're in a strange mood. Not that I mind."

She leaned her back against me and placed her arms up behind my neck, and I soaped off her front, making sure to be very thorough. I still had plenty of soap on the fluffy sponge, so I brushed it against her neck, pressing her head forward. Still with her back to me, I bent her over slightly, washing her with long strokes from her hips to underneath her arms and from the tops of her thighs all the way over her perfect ass and up her spine. I was thorough about washing her behind but even more thorough about rinsing. I had plans for that pulsing opening between her legs.

Bending my knees, I prodded until I easily slipped into her wet channel I was so fond of violating.

"Love you, Shannon," I whispered.

She moaned. "That's how I like it."

"You're the romantic, aren't you?"

"I am. Marco, you feel so good."

We had a slightly longer board meeting in the shower. But she wasn't bored. In fact, by the time we finished, I was ready to discuss more topics. I had a whole drawer full of them, just waiting for me to choose one.

I STOOD AT the end of the dinner table. We'd packed up all the electronics but kept them nearby in case we needed them.

Absalom and Khalil were picked up at the airport just before we were about to begin, but they wanted to go shower after their ordeal. I'd already gotten the report that they'd not been harmed physically, but the expression on their faces told me they'd gotten very seriously shaken up mentally. I'd seen it with hostages many times before, when they'd reach the point that they'd just give up and die.

The boys had only been gone a few hours, but they'd never experienced anything like this, and it horrified them. It was the first lesson of their mentorship. Don't put yourself in a compromising situation with someone you don't know—especially anywhere close to Africa.

So I told them no.

Khalil did a double take. He'd turned and was already heading down the corridor.

"I was tied up all day. I'd like to take a shower."

"I was looking for you all day. We all were, Khalil. Please sit down. We're having a board meeting, and then we'll eat, and then you can take your shower."

He looked at his brother, who didn't react.

"First, a couple announcements. We have three new hires. We have Khalil and Absalom from the Kingdom of Bonin. They are CEOs-in-training. And we have Shannon Marr, weather girl at TMBC in Tampa, who is being hired for strategic planning."

Everyone clapped.

"You boys are being sent by your sultan to learn how to become a successful businessman. Since your particular interest is in housing, we're going to have you work on the Trident Towers, a multifamily housing project on the Gulf of Mexico for disabled and retired Navy SEALs and their dependents. Your father has told me I can put you up in adequate housing of my choosing."

The boys were both stunned. Shannon knew what I was doing but kept a straight face.

I went over some of the ground rules. Forest told the one about swearing double on Fridays. Karin told everyone not to ever bring me a coffee without a lot of cream in it. Paul told the group that Little Bird was my favorite toy and had been responsible for saving many lives over the three years I'd had her. Nigel reminded everyone that football meant soccer and that Americans were getting better, but they really didn't know how to play.

I mentioned that we'd decided to do the project in Florida first before we did Africa. But we were working on obtaining all the permits needed anyway. The ground-breaking would be a way off, though.

Shannon was the troublemaker already. She raised her hand, and I called on her.

"You forgot to give me one."

"Okay, shoot."

"The beach heals everything."

"And that would be correct. You get a gold star today, Shannon. I'll present it to you in private, later."

Everyone laughed.

Absalom raised his hand. "Did Dad really give us to you for a year?"

"You're not slaves. You're going to learn how to

work. You'll be required to run errands, like shopping, and keep your apartments straight. And there will be regular physical fitness things, like swimming and running. You will find that living in Florida won't be anything like living here, but it's not too bad. The weather is a little cooler, but usually less rain."

I told them I was looking for an office building in Tampa, so I would not have anything left in New York or Boston areas. I was going to maintain the leased condo in D.C. That I was divorced from Rebecca and marrying Shannon.

I went over the next few projects and indicated that most of them would center around Florida.

Lastly, I asked everyone to give a high-five to the brothers, who were going to be far from home and living in conditions they were unfamiliar with.

"Someone a long time ago told me that if you wanted to learn something, teach someone. Please help them out as best as you can."

I explained that we would bringing them back to the states on Thursday, but that Shannon and I were staying the full week.

AFTERWARDS, SHANNON AND I went to the sultan's bedroom and were granted an audience. His coloring had improved. I reported that the boys did extremely well, but I knew they'd probably want to talk to him.

"One more item I discussed with Shannon the other night. I wish you two would consider having your wedding here. It would be a week of celebrations, one party after the next. I can honestly say my house puts on the best receptions anywhere on the globe."

"You discussed this?" I asked her, surprised.

"I did. We were busy for a bit, and then I forgot to ask you. I'd be in favor of it, if you are. It would save my folks a lot of money, and it would be spectacular, unlike any wedding either of us have ever attended from pictures I saw.

"Thank you, sir. We'll look at some dates so we can start planning that."

He asked permission to let the boys stay an extra week to spend more time with their mom, in light of the circumstances, and I agreed.

"Now go. I must sleep, but you two go do something fun. And thank you again for bringing my sons home to me. I will forever be in your debt."

"Maybe that was something they had to go through to get their attention. But it's an opportunity, and if they cultivate it and learn from it, some day they may save someone else's life, or possibly their own."

He was going to schedule his doctor visit and would let me know when he was coming for his Boot Camp. I kind of had a logo all picked out for it. I couldn't wait to see him in shorts and flip flops.

WE WERE ENJOYING the warm night. The Tradewinds had shown up, but they were warm tonight.

"My mom and dad used to play this game with Em and I called Best Of. We did it on every vacation, talking about the best of the whole trip," Shannon said.

"I like that idea. What would yours be for this vacation?" I asked.

"Well, it's not over, but I'd have to say the first night, when they made me up in traditional dress, pampered me, and showed me what it was like to live here. They showed me their community and culture and taught me about the power of becoming irresistible."

"That's exactly what you were. What you are."

"What about you?" she asked.

I knew it wasn't going to be as beautiful as the moment Shannon shared with me, but it was my favorite part. And, after all, I was a guy.

"It was all the things in that drawer and what I learned about the power of your love. I hope that, in time, I can make you as happy as you've made me."

Did you enjoy *Unleashed*? The second installment of this book is out now, Restored. And Revenge is coming to you at the end of this month!

Watch for the cover reveal and preorders, which will be going up soon.

This book, like all Sharon's books, will be available in audio format, narrated by J.D. Hart.

You can find out more about this series here. authorsharonhamilton.com/bone-frog-bachelor

If you are a new reader and you want to start with the first SEAL book, Accidental SEAL, the book that launched all the others Sharon has written, as well as the entire series SEAL Brotherhood. You can find them all on her website: authorsharonhamilton.com.

You can listen to most Sharon's book in audio snippets here, all narrated by the talented and award-winning Nashville actor and narrator, J.D. Hart. authorsharonhamilton.com/audiobooks

ABOUT THE AUTHOR

 NYT and USA/Today Bestselling Author Sharon Hamilton's SEAL Brotherhood series have earned her author rankings of #1 in Romantic Suspense, Military Romance and Contemporary Romance. Her other *Brotherhood* stand-alone series are: Bad Boys of SEAL Team 3, Band of Bachelors, True Blue SEALs, Nashville SEALs, Bone Frog Brotherhood, Sunset SEALs, Bone Frog Bachelor Series and SEAL Brotherhood Legacy Series. She is a contributing author to the very popular Shadow SEALs multi-author series.

Her SEALs and former SEALs have invested in two wineries, a lavender farm and a brewery in Sonoma County, which have become part of the new stories. They also have expanded to include Veteran-benefit projects on the Florida Gulf Coast, as well as projects in Africa and the Maldives. One of the SEAL wives has even launched her own women's fiction series. But old characters, as well as children of these SEAL heroes keep returning to all the newer books.

Sharon also writes sexy paranormals in two series: Golden Vampires of Tuscany and The Guardians.

A lifelong organic vegetable and flower gardener, Sharon and her husband lived for fifty years in the Wine Country of Northern California, where many of her stories take place. Recently, they have moved to the beautiful Gulf Coast of Florida, with stories of shipwrecks, the white sugar-sand beaches of Sunset, Treasure Island and Indian Rocks Beaches.

She loves hearing from fans through her website: authorsharonhamilton.com

Find out more about Sharon, her upcoming releases, appearances and news when you sign up for Sharon's newsletter.

Facebook:
facebook.com/SharonHamiltonAuthor

Twitter:
twitter.com/sharonlhamilton

Pinterest:
pinterest.com/AuthorSharonH

Amazon:
amazon.com/Sharon-Hamilton/e/B004FQQMAC

BookBub:
bookbub.com/authors/sharon-hamilton

Youtube:

youtube.com/channel/UCDInkxXFpXp_4Vnq08ZxMBQ

Soundcloud:

soundcloud.com/sharon-hamilton-1

Sharon Hamilton's Rockin' Romance Readers:

facebook.com/groups/sealteamromance

Sharon Hamilton's Goodreads Group:

goodreads.com/group/show/199125-sharon-hamilton-readers-group

Visit Sharon's Online Store:

sharon-hamilton-author.myshopify.com

Join Sharon's Review Teams:

eBook Reviews:

sharonhamiltonassistant@gmail.com

Audio Reviews:

sharonhamiltonassistant@gmail.com

Life is one fool thing after another.
Love is two fool things after each other.

REVIEWS

PRAISE FOR THE
GOLDEN VAMPIRES OF TUSCANY SERIES

"Well to say the least I was thoroughly surprise. I have read many Vampire books, from Ann Rice to Kym Grosso and few other Authors, so yes I do like Vampires, not the super scary ones from the old days, but the new ones are far more interesting far more human than one can remember. I found Honeymoon Bite a totally engrossing book, I was not able to put it down, page after page I found delight, love, understanding, well that is until the bad bad Vamp started being really bad. But seeing someone love another person so much that they would do anything to protect them, well that had me going, then well there was more and for a while I thought it was the end of a beautiful love story that spanned not only time but, spanned Italy and California. Won't divulge how it ended, but I did shed a few tears after screaming but Sharon Hamilton did not let me down, she took me on amazing trip that I loved, look forward to reading another Vampire book of hers."

"An excellent paranormal romance that was exciting, romantic, entertaining and very satisfying to read. It had me anticipating what would happen next many times over, so much so I could not put it down and even finished it up in a day. The vampires in this book were different from your average vampire, but I enjoy different variations and changes to the same old stuff. It made for a more unpredictable read and more adventurous to explore! Vampire lovers, any paranormal readers and even those who love the romance genre will enjoy Honeymoon Bite."

"This is the first non-Seal book of this author's I have read and I loved it. There is a cast-like hierarchy in this vampire community with humans at the very bottom and Golden vampires at the top. Lionel is a dark vampire who are servants of the Goldens. Phoebe is a Golden who has not decided if she will remain human or accept the turning to become a vampire. Either way she and Lionel can never be together since it is forbidden.

I enjoyed this story and I am looking forward to the next installment."

"A hauntingly romantic read. Old love lost and new love found. Family, heart, intrigue and vampires. Grabbed my attention and couldn't put down. Would definitely recommend."

PRAISE FOR THE
SEAL BROTHERHOOD SERIES

"Fans of Navy SEAL romance, I found a new author to feed your addiction. Finely written and loaded delicious with moments, Sharon Hamilton's storytelling satisfies like a thick bar of chocolate." —Marliss Melton, bestselling author of the *Team Twelve* Navy SEALs series

"Sharon Hamilton does an EXCELLENT job of fitting all the characters into a brotherhood of SEALS that may not be real but sure makes you feel that you have entered the circle and security of their world. The stories intertwine with each book before…and each book after and THAT is what makes Sharon Hamilton's SEAL Brotherhood Series so very interesting. You won't want to put down ANY of her books and they will keep you reading into the night when you should be sleeping. Start with this book…and you will not want to stop until you've read the whole series and then…you will be waiting for Sharon to write the next one." (5 Star Review)

"Kyle and Christy explode all over the pages in this first book, *[Accidental SEAL]*, in a whole new series of SEALs. If the twist and turns don't get your heart jumping, then maybe the suspense will. This is a must read for those that are looking for love and adventure with a little sloppy love thrown in for good measure." (5 Star Review)

PRAISE FOR THE
BAD BOYS OF SEAL TEAM 3 SERIES

"I love reading this series! Once you start these books, you can hardly put them down. The mix of romance and suspense keeps you turning the pages one right after another! Can't wait until the next book!" (5 Star Review)

"I love all of Sharon's Seal books, but *[SEAL's Code]* may just be her best to date. Danny and Luci's journey is filled with a wonderful insight into the Native American life. It is a love story that will fill you with warmth and contentment. You will enjoy Danny's journey to become a SEAL and his reasons for it. Good job Sharon!" (5 Star Review)

PRAISE FOR THE
BAND OF BACHELORS SERIES

"*[Lucas]* was the first book in the Band of Bachelors series and it was a phenomenal start. I loved how we got to see the other SEALs we all love and we got a look at Lucas and Marcy. They had an instant attraction, and their love was very intense. This book had it all, suspense, steamy romance, humor, everything you want in a riveting, outstanding read. I can't wait to read the next book in this series." (5 Star Review)

PRAISE FOR THE
TRUE BLUE SEALS SERIES

"Keep the tissues box nearby as you read *True Blue SEALs: Zak* by Sharon Hamilton. I imagine more than I wish to that the circumstances surrounding Zak and Amy are all too real for returning military personnel and their families. Ms. Hamilton has put us right in the middle of struggles and successes that these two high school sweethearts endure. I have read several of Sharon Hamilton's military romances but will say this is the most emotionally intense of the ones that I have read. This is a well-written, realistic story with authentic characters that will have you rooting for them and proud of those who serve to keep us safe. This is an author who writes amazing stories that you love and cry with the characters. Fans of Jessica Scott and Marliss Melton will want to add Sharon Hamilton to their list of realistic military romance writers." (5 Star Review)

"Dear FATHER IN HEAVEN,

If I may respectfully say so sometimes you are a strange God. Though you love all mankind,

It seems you have special predilections too.

You seem to love those men who can stand up alone who face impossible odds, Who challenge every bully and every tyrant ~

Those men who know the heat and loneliness of Calvary. Possibly you cherish men of this stamp because you recognize the mark of your only son in them.

Since this unique group of men known as the SEALs know Calvary and suffering, teach them now the mystery of the resurrection ~ that they are indestructible, that they will live forever because of their deep faith in you.

And when they do come to heaven, may I respectfully warn you, Dear Father, they also know how to celebrate. So please be ready for them when they insert under your pearly gates.

Bless them, their devoted Families and their Country on this glorious occasion.

We ask this through the merits of your Son, Christ Jesus the Lord, Amen."

By Reverend E.J. McMalhon S.J. LCDR, CHC, USN
Awards Ceremony SEAL Team One
1975 At NAB, Coronado

Made in the USA
Coppell, TX
20 August 2022

81796781R00134